WOUNDED FALCON

WOUNDED FALCON

Mary Mackie

Chivers Press • Thorndike Press
Bath, England Waterville, Maine USA

F
MAC

LE MH DB VS HW PW JY EB

This Large Print edition is published by Chivers Press, England, and by Thorndike Press, USA.

Published in 2001 in the U.K. by arrangement with Robert Hale Limited.

Published in 2001 in the U.S. by arrangement with Juliet Burton Literary Agency.

U.K. Hardcover ISBN 0–7540–4591–9 (Chivers Large Print)
U.K. Softcover ISBN 0–7540–4592–7 (Camden Large Print)
U.S. Softcover ISBN 0–7862–3497–0 (General Series Edition)

The text of this Large Print edition is unabridged.
Other aspects of the book may vary from the original edition.

Set in 16 pt. New Times Roman.

Printed in Great Britain on acid-free paper.

British Library Cataloguing in Publication Data available

Library of Congress Cataloging-in-Publication Data

Mackie, Mary.
        Wounded falcon / Mary Mackie.
            p.   cm.
        ISBN 0–7862–3497–0 (lg. print : sc : alk. paper)
        1. Luxembourg—Fiction. 2. Castles—Fiction. 3. Large type books.
I. Title.
PR6063.A2454 W68 2001
823'.914—dc21   2001034665

CHAPTER ONE

On a warm midsummer evening, London's élite gathered for a party at Sharborough House. Countess Sharborough had decreed the occasion to be an 'Edwardian Ball' and most of her guests had obligingly dressed in costume from the early years of the century. Men in white tie and tails, women in satins and lace danced and mingled beneath the glitter of chandeliers.

Among the throng, Julienne Blake moved with her camera, taking pictures of the guests. She was just twenty-three years old, a widow struggling to support herself as a professional photographer; so she was grateful to her godfather and father-in-law, Sir Charles Blake, for recommending her to Lady Sharborough for this occasion.

Charles was here somewhere, 'all done up like a dog's dinner,' as he put it. He had teased Juli about the prim grey gown she was wearing as costume, with her long blonde hair in braids curled round her head—the photographer was disguised as a governess at the behest of Lady Sharborough, just as the waiters all wore footmen's livery, to add to the Edwardian ambience.

As the evening progressed, Juli faintly heard the master of ceremonies announce some late

1

arrivals. The couple appeared in the doorway to the ballroom—a tall man in formal black and white, and beside him the slender figure of the latest 'face' in the modelling world, the stunning eighteen-year-old Eurasian, Lyana. Her idea of Edwardian costume was diaphanous silk of rainbow colours decked with ostrich feathers, hardly authentic but certainly eye-catching.

Protecting her camera as it swung on the strap round her neck, Juli hurriedly squeezed past a knot of guests to where Lyana and her escort were being greeted by their hostess. Lyana made a perfect subject—flawless skin, shining black hair, almond eyes . . .

Having been told to take at least one picture of every guest, Juli next focused her camera on Lyana's escort. As he straightened from bowing over the Countess's hand, he obligingly turned his head and looked straight into the lens.

For Juli, everything stopped—noise, heartbeat, breathing . . . What a glorious man! He was dressed in immaculate white tie and tails, with diamond studs gleaming down the front of his shirt. The formal Edwardian evening wear was a perfect complement to his tall, loose-limbed frame. But all of that was mere periphery to a face that was at once strong and vulnerable, a face of clear-cut lines framed by neat dark hair, with straight brows, classical nose, and a mouth from which the

2

smile was fading as he stared right into Juli's heart and mind with eyes of a clear, brilliant grey.

For one endless moment out of time, only the two of them existed. She was drowning in depthless grey pools in which she could read all his thoughts—and his thoughts were all of her.

Then abruptly sound crashed back. The party returned to life. Music, laughter and strident, chattering voices assailed Juli's ears. Her face flooded with heat as she realised that she had forgotten her camera and was staring at the man over it. He glanced aside, smiling and answering something his lovely companion had said, and as if released from a spell Juli tore herself away. Her palms were sweating and a pulse thudded in her throat in time to her erratic heartbeat. She needed some air.

On the far side of the ballroom, French doors stood open to the night. Juli threaded her way among the guests and gained the cooler air of the terrace, where she drew a long, painful breath. She could still see the man's face as clearly as if he were there beside her. Those bright grey eyes had communicated a great deal. And presumably she had replied with equal clarity; in that moment there had been no room for evasion. They had looked at each other and known . . .

Known what? That they loved? Ridiculous!

Struggling to get a good breath, she leaned

3

on the stone balustrade, fiddling with her camera. It had an automatic wind-on action, but she couldn't remember whether she had taken a photograph of the man or whether her shutter finger had been in suspended animation along with the rest of her. Nothing had been normal in that moment of enchantment.

She stared unseeingly over a garden of trees lit by occasional spotlights. She was trembling uncontrollably, though the June night was caressingly warm. It was crazy to be so affected by a stranger, she told herself angrily. And it was disloyal to her memories of Peter. 'Across a crowded room . . .' It was absurd, a romantic cliché that never happened in real life.

Straightening, she took a deep calming breath of the cool air and determined to stop behaving like some giddy teenager. She was here to do a job, and she would do it.

But the instant she stepped into the ballroom her eyes with a will of their own sought out that certain man and found him dancing with Lyana, who looked small and delicate beside his height. Over the girl's sleek head, his glance met Juli's and she knew that he had been watching for her to reappear. She had not imagined that moment of mutual recognition—he was as aware of her as she was of him.

She went on taking photographs but she found herself keeping track of the movements of one particular man. He danced with his hostess, with other women, then with Lyana again; he stood talking and laughing with a group that included Juli's godfather; and then he took a fresh glass of champagne from the tray of a passing waiter and lifted it in a private toast across the room to Juli with such an impudent smile that she felt her mouth curve in response.

And then, a little later, as she again came near to the terrace doors, a hand locked beneath her elbow and she was impelled out into the mild night air. She didn't need to see him to know whose hand it was. Before she could do more than gasp, he was relieving her of the camera, easing it carefully over her coronet of fair braids.

She knew she ought to make some protest, but every ounce of wit seemed to have deserted her. 'What do you think you're doing?' she asked breathlessly.

'I want to dance with you,' he said, placing the camera in a niche in the wall where it would be safe.

'Guests don't dance with the photographer.'

His laugh came soft as a strong arm round her waist pulled her close to him and he murmured in deep, faintly-accented tones, 'This one does. Don't worry, Miss Prim. No one will see us. You waltz?'

Even if she had never learned how, her feet could have followed his as he swept her into a

5

rhythm to match the music floating from the ballroom. Slowly he drew her further from the lights, into the shadows near the end of the terrace where they were far from other eyes and ears. He leaned a warm cheek on her temple and Juli let her eyelids flicker and close, giving in to the magic that flowed round them in heady, drowsy clouds of unreality.

She began to regret the two glasses of champagne she had accepted from Lady Sharborough. The wine seemed to have dulled her mind but sharpened her senses, which were full of this strong, beautiful man.

'This is crazy,' she muttered.

'This is *wunderbar*,' he argued, his voice deep and blurry as he turned his face a little so that his lips touched her temple. Breaking free was beyond her power. His lips traced a tingling pathway down her cheek and her senses jumped in the moment before his lips caressed the corner of her mouth and she turned unresistingly to meet his kiss.

When he lifted his head, they stared at each other in the shadows. They were no longer dancing but standing close together in the darkness at the end of the terrace, between the bulk of the house and spotlit trees sighing in a night breeze. The mood had altered subtly. All at once, what was happening between them was no longer a game.

'I want to make love to you,' he informed her.

Breathlessly, Juli laughed her disbelief. 'Don't you think we ought to get to know each other first?'

'Doesn't your heart know me already?'

'I don't allow my heart to make decisions like that.'

He tilted a dark eyebrow at her, smiling, his eyes glowing with luminous intensity even in the shadows. 'Perhaps you should.'

Aware that she was in danger of being swept away in the magic of the night and this mesmeric man, Juli said lightly, 'You came with someone else, if you remember.'

'I'm escorting Lyana as a favour to someone,' he informed her.

'How very altruistic of you!' Juli mocked. 'A favour to whom?'

'My mother.'

'Your mother?' She laughed again—unsteadily, nervously. 'I don't believe a word of it.'

He pulled a little face, his smile chiding her. '*Liebchen*, you wound me. Lyana is a beautiful and charming girl—but still a girl, a child. While you, my dear Miss Prim . . .'

His glance had been roaming over her face but now his lashes flickered and dropped and a flush ran over her as she realised he was watching her mouth.

'Before we go any further,' she said, moistening lips that had suddenly gone dry, 'perhaps you should tell me who you are.'

7

But he was already bending over her, murmuring, 'Ask your heart,' as he kissed her with a sweet possessive passion that made the sensible part of her protest, *Crazy! Crazy! In the morning you'll regret this.* But the morning was a lifetime away: the man and the night were her only reality.

A burst of high-pitched laughter made them draw apart as a woman stepped through the ballroom doors some yards away, saying, 'Oh, it's cooler out here! Let's get some air,' and a clutch of people eddied across the terrace amid laughter and chat of the nonsensical kind that occurs in the hours after midnight when champagne has been flowing.

A slender figure in feathers and silks detached itself from the group and came gliding along the terrace. Juli saw that it was Lyana; her long black hair flowed over one shoulder in a shining swathe as she lifted her beautiful pale face and almond eyes to smile at Juli's companion. 'I've been looking for you everywhere, Andreas. I think we should go now. We have a plane to catch tomorrow at ten, if you remember. I need my beauty sleep.'

'I'll be with you in a few moments,' he promised.

'Very well.' Lyana glanced at Juli, with what appeared to be mild curiosity and . . . was there a hint of amusement in those liquid dark eyes? Before Juli could decide, Lyana turned on her heel and walked gracefully away.

8

'A plane?' Juli queried as casually as she could when chill reality was beginning to dispel her illusions. 'To where?'

'New York,' he replied.

She received the news in silence, feeling that words might choke her. Then she said in a flat, brittle voice, 'How nice for you. I suppose you're making the trip as another favour to your mother?'

'You might say that.'

Angry now—mostly with her own gullibility—she began to turn away, but he caught her hand and held it in a purposeful manner. When Juli glanced back at him she saw a corner of his mouth curve ruefully. 'Do you believe in fate?' he asked.

She shook her head, hating him. 'No. No, I don't think I do.'

'Then you're wrong, *Liebchen*. Some day we shall meet again, you and I. And then you will apologise for the unkind things you're thinking about me now.'

'I won't hold my breath,' she retorted.

Before she could move, he had bent and brushed a swift kiss across her mouth and then he was gone, leaving her confused. The memory of him lingered in her senses, and in the mouth that tingled from the touch of his. Whoever and whatever he was, she was branded by the lightning that had sparked between them.

*   *   *

Though people remembered seeing the dark-haired man, none of them knew his identity; he had been Lyana's escort and Lyana had called him Andreas: that was all they knew. When Juli asked her godfather if he had discovered the name of the man with whom he had briefly chatted, Charles's twinkling eyes assessed her shrewdly.

'Why are you so keen to know? Fancied him, did you? My darling Juli, if he's the type of man who trails model girls on his arm then he's not for you. A gigolo. A libertine. A Lothario.' He rolled his eyes at her under bushy brows, enlarging on the theme with relish, 'A rakehell! And—what is worse—a foreigner, too.'

'I'm part foreign myself,' she reminded him.

'Oh, being half French doesn't count,' Charles averred. 'You were born and raised in England, that's what matters. This chap was pure Teuton. Not your type at all. All the same, I'm relieved to know you're beginning to take an interest in men again.'

'It's not like that!' Juli objected. 'I just thought he had a photogenic face. Of course I didn't "fancy" him, Charles. Anyway, I thought you disliked that phrase.'

'I hate all your modern slang,' Charles said, smiling at her, though she could see the sorrow behind his eyes. 'And don't try to put me off

10

the scent, Juli girl. Maybe this chap wasn't the one, but someone will come along some day. It's only natural. Peter wouldn't have wanted you to spend all your life grieving for him, you know.'

She could think of no reply to that. In his way, he was telling her that he would try not to mind when a man came along who could take Peter's place in her life. Which was generous of him, because Peter had been his only son.

Without need for words, she reached to kiss his cheek and share a smile of total empathy with him. He was such a darling with his kindly, smiley face and the crisp, crinkly hair that had once been black but was now liberally threaded with silver. Since her parents had died when she was twelve years old, Juli had learned to depend on Charles's loyal support. Marrying Charles's son, her childhood sweetheart, when she was barely nineteen, had been the most natural thing in the world.

When Peter died so suddenly, in an accident while rock-climbing less than two years after their marriage, Juli's life had been shattered again. She couldn't imagine what she would ever have done without Charles. In their mutual grief they had leaned on each other for comfort. Together, they had picked up the pieces of their lives. He still watched over her, worried about her . . .

Now, he patted her shoulder, embarrassed by the emotion of the moment. 'Come on, let

11

me take you home. It's all very well for you to look fresh as a daisy at three a.m., Juli girl, but old chaps like me need their beauty sleep.'

*　　　*　　　*

For a while Juli remained disturbed by her memories of the man named Andreas. When her phone rang she half expected that he might be calling her. She wasted hours imagining a reunion with him, though the rational part of her mind knew she would never see him again.

But she did keep a memento of that night—a picture of a dark-haired man with brilliant grey eyes and a mouth that curved on the edge of a smile. She hid the photograph away where only she could see it. When life got too mundane, that picture was a reminder that once there had been a wildly romantic evening when fantasies came to life.

The pictures of the party came out well and Lady Sharborough began to recommend Juli's services to her friends and contacts. Juli worked hard at building her career, accepting any assignment that came her way as she gradually became known in her field. Her career blossomed.

But her personal life was less fulfilled; she retained her close links with Charles and she had friends, but no man came near to breaking down her barriers of reserve. She might have thought that her capacity for love had died with Peter, except that she still recalled how a charismatic stranger had effortlessly swept aside all her defences one mad midsummer night.

As the weeks and then the months passed, the incident faded in her memory, becoming like something she must have imagined. Juli had a life to live, a career to follow. She was much too busy to brood over impossible dreams.

* * *

On a February evening some two and a half years after that ball at Sharborough House, Juli was busy in her darkroom when her doorbell began to shrill impatiently. Irritated, Juli left the red-lit room, shouting, 'All right! All right!'

Beyond the window of her sitting-room, the lights of London shone mistily across the dark Thames, but they vanished as she switched on the light and the view was obscured behind layers of chiffon drapes. Blinking in the brightness, she went to answer the bell.

In the hallway outside her door, a pile of brand-new clothing met her eyes. Howard Marston was holding the garments; she could just see his fair hair and blue eyes whose expression said he was about to collapse under the burden as he groaned, 'Let me in, Jules.'

She stepped back, letting him stagger into the flat to dump his burden across a settee. Sighing in relief, he hurriedly began to shake creases out of the clothes and hang them on door edges and picture rail. They were all outfits bearing his own label, 'HM'.

'Just what,' said Juli, 'is going on? Have your workshops been affected by a plague of water, or is it a flood of mice?'

Howard pulled a face at her. 'You're always such a comfort. Oh, Lord . . .' He noticed her stained overall and the faint smell of chemicals that hung about her. 'Were you working?'

'You should be a detective,' said Juli, shaking out the cap of golden-blonde hair which she now wore short for convenience. 'Howard, what is this all about? You turn up at my door at nine-thirty at night, demand to be let in, litter my tidy flat with rags and—'

'Ouch!' Howard winced to hear his creations described in such scathing terms, and turned cajoling: 'Darling Jules . . .'

She had heard that tone of voice before. 'Whatever it is . . . No.'

Howard merely stood there looking forlorn. He was in his early thirties, tall and slim with curly fair hair and the bluest of eyes. He was an attractive man, and had become a good friend. Normally Juli was pleased of his company.

Just at this moment, however, he was a nuisance.

14

'It's this Luxembourg trip,' he said with a gesture of little-boy helplessness. 'With all the snags that have cropped up over the big charity show next week, I can't spare the time to go. So I wondered if *you* . . .'

'Oh, Howard, no!' Juli groaned. 'Just when I thought I'd got a few days to myself for a change! There must be someone else.'

'There isn't. Well, nobody I trust to do the job properly. It's important, Jules.'

A reminder buzzer was sounding from her darkroom. 'And so are my pictures,' she said, making for the inner door.

Howard followed her into the red-lit room where enlargements were processing in trays of fluid. She removed them carefully, examining them before hanging them up to dry, while Howard moved restlessly about, his mind on his own problem.

'The thing is, you see,' he went on, 'I can't afford to offend the von Remmens. Besides their involvement in heavy industry and whatever, they've got an interest in a chain of boutiques across Europe. Imagine it— 'Howard Marston. London, Paris, Rome . . .'

'So there's method in your madness, is there?' Juli commented.

'Of course there is. I'm in business, Jules. A contact with Madame Ghislaine could be very useful. Look . . . I had to do a lot of hard talking to get the old girl to agree to our using her home as a background, and then she had

15

to get the approval of her son—who's the boss of the outfit. Since they've now been kind enough to invite me on a preliminary visit, I can't offend them by refusing. And you *are* going to be the photographer on the session in April. You can do it, Jules. Just roll those big blue eyes . . .'

'My eyes aren't blue,' Juli objected, switching on the normal white light.

Howard threw up a hand to shade his eyes, peering at her and pleading, 'You'll do it for me, won't you?'

'Well . . .' she demurred, weakening.

'Bless you!' He moved swiftly around the bench and caught her waist, leaning to kiss her cheek. 'You're an angel.'

'I'm an idiot,' she retorted. 'You think you can sweet-talk me into anything.'

'I wish that were true. I'd sweet-talk you to the altar. You know I love you madly. If I thought . . .'

The words trailed off as he stared beyond her and reached suddenly for the framed photograph she kept on a shelf among stacks of printing paper. The glossy print showed a man in evening dress, a vibrantly attractive man with dark hair and smiling grey eyes.

'Hello!' Howard muttered, frowning over the picture. 'Who the devil is this?'

Juli only just prevented herself from snatching the frame out of his hands. Despite herself, the sight of that beautiful masculine

16

face filled her with a bittersweet nostalgia she ought to have grown out of by now. She recalled the mesmeric quality of those bright grey eyes, and the trace of accent in that deep, musical voice. Even the memory sent shivers down her spine.

Two and a half years had passed since that evening at Sharborough House, she reminded herself. It was part of the past. Finished with.

Even so, the memories remained vivid and oddly disturbing.

Feigning indifference, she took the photograph from Howard and laid it face-down on the shelf.

'It's nobody,' she lied. 'Just someone I saw once. I was rather pleased with the way the picture came out, so I kept it, that's all. Now come and tell me what all these clothes are for.'

The ploy to distract his attention from the photograph succeeded. Howard followed her into the sitting-room where the selection of high-fashion outfits graced plain white walls and flower-printed couches.

'They're for you,' he said.

'For me?' she queried in astonishment. 'Whatever for?'

'For you to wear while you're at Falkenruhe. I want you to impress Madame Ghislaine with them—show her how my clothes look on a real woman, in a real setting. They're all your size. Just take your pick.'

Juli sighed to herself. 'You're taking a great deal for granted.'

'I know,' said Howard, unabashed. 'But you're much too sweet to refuse me. Besides, you're a woman, and you can't deny you like having pretty things to wear. It'll only be for a couple of days, Jules. The break might do you the world of good.' Looking unusually serious, he laid his hands on her shoulders and leaned to press a kiss on her brow before looking at her with affectionate blue eyes. 'If you stay here you'll only find things to do—in that darkroom, or rushing about after old Charles. You've lost the knack of relaxing, Juli.'

She squinted at him suspiciously, reminded of a conversation she had had with her godfather. 'You've been talking to Charles!'

'Yes, I have, and we're both concerned about you. You work too hard. But now's your chance to enjoy a few days' luxury. Madame Ghislaine is charming. I've only spoken to her son on the phone, but he sounds nice, too, though . . . come to think of it, I hope he's not *too* nice. I want you back.' He studied her face for a moment, then said, 'You're right, your eyes aren't blue. They're sort of tawny-hazel. And they're beautiful. Like you,' with which he kissed her full on her lips.

Juli did not resist him but her response was perfunctory and after a moment Howard drew back, smiling wryly. He knew that all she felt for him was affection and though he would

18

have liked it to be more he never pushed or made demands.

'So when do I leave?' she asked.

Howard slid her a shame-faced look from his eye corner. 'Tomorrow, actually.'

'Tomorrow?!' Juli exclaimed in exasperation. 'But that means I shall have to . . . Oh, Howard . . . You're a monster!'

* * *

Lights were beginning to wink in February dusk as Juli stood waiting on the concourse of the airport, her high-heeled boots planted either side of her suitcase. The transition from London to Luxembourg City had been accomplished in such a rush that she still felt dazed.

Easing the strap of her shoulder-bag, she stuffed her hands into the roomy pockets of the grey blouson jacket that matched a calf-length skirt. The outfit had blue touches at collar, cuffs and seams, echoing the plaid of the long scarf that draped round her neck—a Howard Marston design, of course. Despite her show of reluctance, she was delighted with the chance to wear clothes that were beyond her usual budget. And Howard had been right; a couple of days away would do her good.

'Ms Blake?' A man had paused beside her, dressed in chauffeur's uniform of pine-green, complete with peaked cap. 'Herr von Remmen

19

is waiting in the car,' he informed her in guttural English, bending to slide the case out from between her feet. 'Please follow me.'

Outside, the daylight was fading and lights brightened over a thin covering of snow that was beginning to sparkle as the temperature fell. Treading carefully so as not to slip in her high-heeled boots, Juli followed the chauffeur to where a sleek and shining Mercedes limousine was parked.

As the chauffeur opened the rear door and the interior light came on, Juli stopped dead in the act of ducking into the car. Her heart jumped and suddenly her pulses were racing as if she had been running.

The man who occupied the far side of the rear seat was not the stranger she had expected. Instead, he was achingly familiar. She had last seen him in the flesh on a June evening at Sharborough House, two years, seven months and nineteen days before!

He was dressed in a tailored black topcoat that hung open over a business suit. He looked a little older, a little thinner, but he still had the power to accelerate her heartbeat. She remembered every line of those strong features and straight brows under a sweep of dark hair against which his grey eyes looked startlingly clear. Surely he must know her, too?

But not the least flicker of recognition troubled his calm, questioning expression. The brilliant grey eyes seemed to be looking right

20

through her with an intensity that raised all the tiny hairs on her nape.

'Ms Blake,' he greeted her politely, holding out a hand in greeting. 'I am Andreas von Remmen. Welcome to Luxembourg. Please, join me.'

CHAPTER TWO

Having closed her into the warmth of the car, the chauffeur stowed Juli's case in the boot and took his place behind the wheel, beyond a glass partition that gave his passengers privacy. From her corner of the shadows that now filled the car, Juli stole another glance at her companion. Andreas . . . Andreas von Remmen. It was incredible.

He was settling himself more comfortably in the back of the seat, an arm stretched along the base of the window. His profile was etched against distant lights, still impossibly familiar to her. Memories of a night of unbearable awareness came swarming around her.

But obviously the sight of her had stirred no similar memories for him. Well, what else had she expected? She had been just another night's flirtation for him.

The car had moved off, heading from brightly lit streets to the sweep of lights on an autoroute.

'How was the flight?' he asked.

Making a conscious effort for normality, Juli said, 'Not bad. Though I wouldn't say it's my favourite method of travelling.'

'Nor mine. However hard one tries to relax, one always arrives feeling crumpled and irritable.'

'Yes, that's right.'

Realising what he had said, he half turned toward her, saying, 'I didn't mean . . . I'm sure you're not crumpled—or irritable.'

'I'm a little of both,' Juli confessed.

'Then . . . perhaps you would enjoy a glass of wine.' Without waiting for a reply he leaned to open a lighted, refrigerated cocktail cabinet containing glasses and a bottle of white wine whose cork had already been loosened. 'It's from our own vineyard,' he said. 'A Himmelstein Riesling. Quite dry. Does that suit you?'

'Very much so. Thank you.'

As he poured some of the chilled wine into a glass, she found herself fascinated by the strong, shapely hands that were clearly visible in the light from the cabinet. Once, those hands had touched her as he held her in his arms and pressed passionately close. *Your heart knows me*, he had said, the sweet-talking liar!

Having given her a glass and filled one for himself, he lifted it in a brief toast. *'Prosit!'*

'Santé,' Juli replied, sipping the wine, which proved to be light, flowery and refreshing. She sighed in appreciation. 'That's good.'

'We think so,' Andreas agreed. 'You know wine, Ms Blake?'

'I'm afraid I'm no connoisseur. I didn't realise you had vineyards, but then I don't know much about Luxembourg, except that I've been told the Ardennes district is very

23

beautiful.'

'Yes, it's beautiful,' he agreed, 'and full of history. I hope you'll find Falkenruhe suitable for your pictures. You're planning to photograph a range of Howard Marston clothes, I understand.'

'Yes, and . . . I'm sorry, I should have said . . . Howard asked me to apologise for him. He intended to come himself but at the last minute there were problems over a charity fashion show he's organising. The Princess of Wales will be there, so naturally he wants it to go as smoothly as possible.'

'So he explained over the phone,' came the calm reply. 'It's fortunate you were available to deputise for him, Ms Blake.'

'I happened to be between commissions, and since I'm the one who'll be taking the pictures in April . . .' She hesitated, recalling that she had been taking pictures the night they met. 'Of course when we actually fly over with the models hopefully the weather will be better. Howard wants to catch the spring leaves and blossom.'

'Then April should be ideal,' Andreas said. 'I'm told that Mr Marston is a talented designer.'

'Yes, he is. At least, the fashion world seems to think so.'

'I'm afraid,' Andreas said ruefully, 'that my knowledge of fashion is on a par with your knowledge of wine, Ms Blake.'

24

'You mean, you know what you like, when you see it?'

There was the slightest awkward pause, making Juli wonder what nerve she had touched, then he answered smoothly enough, 'In a way. But my mother claims to have perfect taste. No doubt she will enjoy talking clothes with you.'

'I hope I shan't disappoint her. After all, my business is photography, not fashion. But I know Howard considers Madame Ghislaine to be one of the arbiters of European taste.'

'I'm sure she will be delighted to hear it,' Andreas said with a touch of dry humour.

She was vividly aware of being alone with him, in warm darkness touched by passing lights. When he spoke, his voice caressed her, deep and soft, with only the slightest foreign inflection. What kind of man was he? Amoral and hedonistic, as Charles had labelled him, and as her own common sense assured her? Unfortunately her reasoning processes were confused by her instinctive female response to the vibrant reality of the man.

'It was kind of you to meet me,' she said into the silence. 'I hope I didn't cause you any inconvenience.'

'No, on the contrary,' Andreas replied. 'I was in the city anyway. Our main office is there. As a rule, I commute from Falkenruhe.'

'Falkenruhe . . .' she repeated, making conversation. 'Is that the village, or the house?'

'It's the mountain,' he told her. 'Down long ages there have been falcons nesting on the cliff. Falkenruhe means "the place of falcons". You speak German?'

'A little.' She glanced at him in dismay. 'But I thought the official language here was French.'

'So it is. But the most common spoken language is Letzburgish, which is a high German dialect.'

It all sounded rather confusing. 'Then I'm relieved you speak such good English.'

'In international business, it's necessary. And, since my mother was born in France, at home we tend to mix languages. German, French, English . . .'

'Then I shall be able to communicate,' Juli said in relief. 'I'm half French myself. I spent a lot of childhood holidays with my grandparents in Nancy. What part of France is your mother from?'

'From Paris itself. She has an apartment there. But at present she's staying at Falkenruhe. She feels that she is needed.'

'Oh?'

'My brother died suddenly last spring—of meningitis,' he informed her. 'His wife and his son live at Falkenruhe now.'

'Oh, I—I'm sorry.'

'Yes, Ms Blake, it was a tragedy. He was only thirty years old.'

Despite the words, he sounded almost unmoved by his brother's fate, or was it just that he was being so horribly stiff and formal? She wished he would not keep calling her 'Ms' Blake—she disliked that ugly modernism and it was beginning to grate on her.

'So my mother remains at Falkenruhe,' he went on, 'to be near Sara and young Karl. At such times, a family should be together.'

'Of course. I only hope my visit won't be an intrusion.'

'You will provide a welcome relief, Ms Blake. Nine months of gloom is enough. I'm sure Heini—my brother—would have hated it.'

'Would you . . . Would you mind not calling me Ms Blake?' Juli asked. 'It sounds so ugly and contrived.'

He shifted in his seat, as if he had cramp from keeping still so long. 'Forgive me. I dislike the term myself. If I were a woman I too might object to being addressed as though I were an angry bee. It shall be *Miss* Blake, then.'

'Strictly speaking, it's Mrs.'

He jerked his head towards her and she saw his eyes glimmering in the shadows as he said sharply, 'You're married?'

'I was. I've been a widow for almost five years now.'

To this, Andreas made no reply.

How close he was in the darkness. If she

were to reach out only a little way, she could touch him. The awareness made her feel hot.

'And you?' she heard herself say unguardedly.

'I?'

'You have a wife?'

'Ah . . .' He exhaled audibly, though whether in a sigh or a cynical laugh she couldn't tell. 'No, not any more, Ms . . . Mrs Blake. My wife divorced me two years ago.'

'Oh. I . . . I see.'

This feeble response hung awkwardly between them and Juli cursed herself for not finding something more original to say. But she was thrown by the conflicting emotions his statement had aroused. He must have been married when they first met, yet he had openly been running around with a young model, and making casual passes at ingenuous lady photographers along the way. Didn't he have any scruples at all?

In the silence, the car's engine purred smoothly, carrying them along a road where trees leaned out with bare branches to touch other trees overhead, forming a tunnel through which the headlamps cut a bright swathe. Juli stared at the laced branches swiftly passing in the night. The journey had taken on a dreamlike quality. Was she actually riding through the darkness with a stranger who once, in some other existence, had taken her heart and soul by storm? It was unreal.

*　　*　　*

They left the autobahn and came to a twisting valley road where small towns nestled amid forested hills. In the light of streetlamps, Juli saw tall grey buildings trimmed with windowboxes and shutters. Ancient churches and half-timbered town halls flanked cobbled market squares where cars were parked and people headed homeward, wrapped up against the cold. Soon the Mercedes turned on to a narrower side road affording glimpses of a floodlit castle high on a hill ahead. The car climbed steadily through an old village of narrow, winding streets, coming to a steep lane that led up beneath overhanging trees. At length the headlamps picked out an ancient, weathered archway, beyond which lay a courtyard and the ivy-clung walls of the castle Juli had glimpsed from below. To her surprise, the car slowed and eased in under the archway.

The grandeur of the place took her breath away. Bathed in light from hidden floodlamps, its towering turrets rose over walls in which the windows were buried deep among ivy, and its door was reached by a flight of broad stone steps that curved up the angle of the hillside from the courtyard.

'Is this where you live?' she asked as the car slid to a halt at the foot of the steps.

'This is Falkenruhe, yes.'

The chauffeur was getting out, opening the door near his employer and saying something in German about ice Andreas ducked out of the vehicle and turned to offer a helping hand to Juli, saying, 'There's ice on the ground. Be careful.'

She wasn't sure which affected her most—the warm touch of his hand as he helped her from the car, or the imposing floodlit castle that irresistibly drew her eyes. It appeared to be painted in colours of ivy-green and warm golden stone against a sky full of frosty stars.

A sigh of sheer enchantment was drawn from her. 'Oh, my!'

'You like it?' Andreas asked.

'It's the most beautiful place I've seen in my life.'

As he released her hand she started to move away, only to feel her foot slip on the frozen ground. She grasped instinctively at Andreas's coat to save herself from falling, but cannoned into him, almost unbalancing him. She felt him take hold of her arms, steadying himself and supporting her as she righted herself on awkward high heels, dazed by that momentary contact with him even through thick winter clothing.

'I'm sorry,' she gasped, her face burning as she looked up at him and saw him smile tightly, his grey eyes vague and unfocused, staring through her unseeingly, as they had at the airport.

Unseeing . . . Oh—dear God!

'I warned you of the ice,' he said, his fingers still hard around her upper arms as if he were afraid she might slip again. 'The steps will be treacherous. Forgive me, but I must pass to Franz the duty of looking after you. He will escort you safely to the door. Franz . . .'

The chauffeur laid a hand under Juli's elbow, drawing her away, but for a moment she resisted, sick with horror and sympathy as she watched the way Andreas felt for the car door and reached inside to retrieve his briefcase. He had covered the disability well; in the shadows of the car she would never have guessed.

But it was true, just the same—Andreas von Remmen was blind.

*   *   *

Wrapped in an enormous fluffy towel, Juli stared into the steamy bathroom mirror. She had been so distracted by her thoughts that she hadn't taken much note of the castle through which she had been brought by a uniformed maid. She remembered a confusion of rooms, corridors and stairs, rococo ceilings, baroque furniture. Her guest suite had an oak four-poster, draped with rich brocade; the bathroom boasted gold-plated taps. Clearly the von Remmens wanted for nothing.

Except that Andreas couldn't see. Her thoughts kept returning to that fact, rediscovering it each time with a cold shock of dismay.

She returned to the bedroom still wrapped in the bath towel, to find a plump red-cheeked maid unpacking her case. They greeted each other and then, since the maid spoke no English, Juli tried out her halting German and discovered that the maid's name was Beata, and that dinner would be served at eight.

Mostly through gestures, Juli asked what she should wear for the evening, and Beata picked out a long skirt, a rustling black taffeta on which were printed deep pink peonies. Obviously, at Falkenruhe, the von Remmens dressed for dinner.

To go with the skirt, Howard had supplied a pink cashmere jumper whose neckline dipped at the back into a deep scoop. Juli hoped the castle was properly heated. She took care over her make-up and added ear-rings and necklace of huge fake pink pearls. Her short-cropped hair gleamed gold in the light and she thought Howard would be proud of her, but sadly the one person whose opinion really mattered to her was the one person to whom her looks were no longer of any importance. Andreas would hear her, probably smell her perfume, possibly even touch her. But he wouldn't see her.

Imagining how it must be for him, Juli felt a

lump rise in her throat and her eyes stung with tears. Though common sense told her that on the evening they met he had been flirting outrageously and she had been a fool even to half believe him, still she did not believe he had intended any real harm. It had been a joke, that was all—a fairy-tale come briefly to life with herself as Cinderella. But whatever trauma had robbed Andreas of his sight, it had changed him; he was no longer the lively, laughing, carefree man who had woven midsummer enchantment for a girl who had badly needed a dream to cling to.

A soft tapping sounded at her door and an equally soft female voice called, 'Mrs Blake?'

'Come in,' Juli replied, and watched curiously as the door opened and a young woman peered round, a nervous smile lighting a pretty face framed in long auburn hair.

'I'm Sara. I'm, er, Andreas's sister-in-law,' she informed Juli as she came fully into the room with an almost apologetic air. 'I thought you might like a guide to get you down to the dining-room.'

'How thoughtful of you!' Juli laughed. 'Yes, I've been thinking I should need a map to find my way. But . . . you're English.'

'Yes.' Sara blushed self-consciously. She appeared to be in her early twenties, and she was painfully thin in a figure-hugging velvet dress of midnight blue. Her face was pale and Juli suspected she had been crying.

Of course, she remembered, Sara had lost her young husband only nine months ago. Juli knew how deeply bereavement could hurt. It had taken her years to get over losing Peter—if one ever recovered from that sort of pain.

'To be honest,' Sara was saying, 'I still feel a bit lost here myself. Heini and I had a flat in Luxembourg City. I wish they'd let me go back, but . . . well, you know how it is.'

'I expect they're afraid you might be lonely,' Juli said.

Sara watched her for a moment, the expression in her green eyes almost cynical. 'No, it's not that,' she said, but didn't explain. 'Well, are you ready? We'd better go. Madame Ghislaine hates people being late.'

The castle appeared like a labyrinth, but at length the corridors, lit by pools of light, led to an elegant stairway curving down to a hall lined with bookcases and suits of armour. Another broader corridor, panelled in fruitwood from floor to ceiling, provided access to more rooms, one door standing open so that Juli heard Andreas speaking in French to a woman who replied in the same language.

As they approached that door, Sara glanced round to say in an undertone laced with brittle humour, 'Got your armour well buckled? Into the fray!'

*   *   *

The 'small' sitting-room contained armchairs and settees grouped for conversation around antique tables bearing Chinese vases full of dried flowers. It was mainly blue and white, the oriental theme continued in fabrics and decoration, and porcelain displayed in glass cabinets. A huge fireplace formed the focal point on that February evening, with flames leaping round a pile of logs.

But the room was only a setting for the people who inhabited it. Juli's glance went at once to the tall form of Andreas, now wearing a dinner jacket and black bow tie, with dark glasses to hide his eyes. He was leaning on the mantelpiece, one hand in his pocket and his dark head bent attentively as he conversed with the woman who sat in a wing chair by the fire. She looked round as Sara and Juli went in.

'Ah, here is our visitor!' she cried. 'And Sara. Good evening, my dear.'

Murmuring, *'Maman,'* Sara hurried to kiss the lifted cheek.

Madame Ghislaine held out a thin, elegant hand to Juli. 'Mrs Blake. Welcome to Falkenruhe.'

Conscious of the skirt rustling around her, Juli moved across the room to shake hands. Madame Ghislaine was still a beauty, her grey hair drawn into a soft chignon that flattered her oval face with its aristocratic nose, and her thin figure was clad in a gown of wine-red silk.

35

A diamond necklace glittered at her throat, matching the jewels on her hands.

'How exquisite you look,' Madame complimented Juli. 'Is that one of Mr Marston's creations? He's to be congratulated. But of course you do it full justice. You should be in front of the camera, not behind it. Sit down, my dear—and you too, Sara. Don't hover like that. Is Karl asleep?'

'He was when I left the nursery,' Sara said, taking herself to a chair in a shadowed corner, as if she preferred to stay out of the conversation.

A wave of one of those beringed hands brought Franz from his place by the door to a cocktail cupboard. He had changed his uniform for a suit, and presumably his role from chauffeur to butler. He served drinks with quiet efficiency.

Aware of Andreas standing silent, listening with a half-smile on his lips, and with those awful dark glasses covering his eyes, Juli perched on the edge of a settee, accepting a glass of wine from Franz.

'Well, you are quite a surprise!' Madame Ghislaine informed her. 'Not only were we expecting Mr Marston—until this morning— but his photographer proves to be an attractive young woman. I have always thought the idea was for the fashion photographer to flirt with his models to bring out the best in them. It can hardly be so with a woman behind the camera.'

'It's the camera they play to, Madame, not the person behind it,' Juli said.

'You think so? But a little interplay between the sexes adds a certain piquancy—a certain sparkle—wouldn't you say?'

'It doesn't make any difference, in my experience, not if the model's a professional.'

Exquisitely arched eyebrows rose the merest fraction, managing to express reproof; evidently Madame was not accustomed to being argued with.

She turned the conversation to Howard Marston and his recent rise to wider fame in the fashion world, then began to quiz Juli about her own career—a subject which continued over dinner.

The blue dining-room was obviously a family room, though quite large enough to hold a table that would seat twelve, plus ornate sideboards and a glass cabinet displaying magnificent crystal pieces. The food was equally rich, served by Beata and another maid—a strong game paté with French toast, trout with almonds, veal cutlets in a thick wine sauce, apple strudel laced with brown sugar, and finally cheese, fruit and nuts. With every course came an appropriate wine, of which Juli took only a little; she ate sparingly, too, asking for small portions.

Throughout the meal, Franz was a discreet presence hovering at Andreas's shoulder to help him when necessary, but it was done without fuss. Andreas coped calmly, joining in the conversation occasionally, though his mother dominated the table. He seemed to be indulging her, letting her ramble on to Juli about clothes and about France while he ate his meal in peace. As for Sara, she said hardly a word, ate very little, but drank freely of the wine that was available.

Just as Franz was enquiring whether he should serve coffee, Sara gave a great moaning sigh and pushed herself unsteadily to her feet, muttering, 'I can't stay awake any longer. I'm so tired! Excuse me.' She staggered from the room and Juli glimpsed a maid who seemed to have been waiting to take charge of the girl.

'We shall take coffee in the small sitting-room,' Madame announced, laying aside her napkin and pushing back her chair as though nothing had happened. 'Andreas—your arm.'

'Is Sara all right?' he asked, not moving to obey the summons.

His mother replied in rapid German that Juli couldn't follow, except that the dismissive, long-suffering tone of Madame's voice was unmistakable. Obviously she didn't care much for her daughter-in-law and, just as obviously, so it seemed to Juli, Sara was a miserably unhappy young woman.

After they returned to the sitting-room, Madame herself poured coffee, enthroned in her wing chair, while Andreas and Juli shared a settee, with three feet of blue pagoda-printed velvet between them.

'I hope you'll excuse our little Sara,' Madame said. 'She has taken it all very badly, I'm afraid. She forgets that we miss Heini, too. He was my baby, my younger son, and Andreas's only brother.'

'But Sara was his wife,' Andreas added. 'She's very young, and with a child to bring up. She feels it most.'

Madame's expression said she doubted that, but whatever she was thinking she kept it to herself. The subject of Sara was dropped.

Having drunk one small cup of coffee, Madame decided it was time she retired to her room. Her son rose politely to his feet and Juli found herself copying him—Madame Ghislaine tended to have that effect on people, as if she were royalty. She shook Juli's hand, reached to kiss Andreas's cheek, and made for the door, where she turned to say, 'I shall look in on Sara. *Bonne nuit, mes enfants.*'

Andreas resumed his seat, shaking his head. 'She has said the same thing for as long as I can remember—good night, my children. To her I shall never be full grown.'

'That's the way with mothers,' Juli said, remaining on her feet, reluctant to sit near to him now that they were alone.

'Yours is the same?' he asked.

'I expect she would have been. My parents both died when I was twelve, so I never found out. But my godfather still treats me as if I were a little girl. Herr von Remmen . . . may I help myself to more coffee?'

'Please do. And some for me, too. What did I do with my cup?'

The cup was on the floor not far from his feet. Taffeta skirt whispering, Juli bent to pick it up, but as she reached for the cup her fingers tangled with his searching hand and were caught, gently but insistently. Feeling hot, she looked up into his face, seeing her own twin reflection in the dark mirror-glasses.

'You must resist the temptation to help me, Mrs Blake,' he said in a low voice that caused a ripple of unease and delight to run down her spine, reminding her that her back was exposed to the air. 'I'm not helpless. Very far from it.'

'I'm sorry.' The words were a whisper. She could hardly breathe for his nearness and when his free hand lifted and touched her face she had to bite her lip to prevent herself from exclaiming aloud. His fingers struck fire from her skin, waking every tiny nerve as he brushed a long thumb across her lips as if to silence her.

'No, don't apologise,' he said. 'I understand. But *you* must understand that it irritates me not to be allowed to do everything I am still capable of doing, however trivial. Even picking up a cup.'

For a breathless moment, neither of them moved. Awareness flared between them and he carefully removed his hand from her face, slowly unclasping the fingers that held hers, as if he had only just realised what he was doing.

'Forgive me.'

'For what?' Juli asked with a laugh that came false as a cracked bell. Hurriedly, she stood up. 'I'll pour the coffee, if you'll hand me your cup.'

He did so and she knelt by the low table, trembling so much that the stream of coffee from the pot almost splattered into the saucer.

'Sometimes,' Andreas said, 'the urge to let my fingers see for me becomes too strong to resist. If I embarrassed you, I apologise.'

'You didn't embarrass me,' she lied. 'Here's your coffee.' She placed the cup in his outstretched hand, taking care not to touch him.

Sitting on the hearthrug with the warmth from the fire caressing her bare shoulders, she watched him with wide, troubled eyes, studying the way his hair grew to fall across his brow. Tonight, in evening clothes, he looked very much as he had the night they had met at Sharborough House, except for the dark glasses that were a bleak reminder of the changes in him.

She wanted very much to tell him they had met before, but uncertainty made her silent. Most probably he would not remember the incident. He had been married, at the time, but still he had been flaunting a teenaged beauty on his arm. What else could Juli have been but a brief diversion for him?

41

CHAPTER THREE

'Don't watch me,' Andreas said suddenly. 'I can feel your eyes on me. What are you thinking behind that silence?'

'I . . . I was admiring the room,' Juli prevaricated. 'You have a lovely home.'

'Thank you. And what is your home like?'

'Mine?' She laughed to herself at the comparison. 'I have a studio flat in a converted warehouse, by the Thames.'

'You live alone?' he asked.

'Why . . . yes.'

'You said you had lost your parents,' he recalled. 'Have you no family at all?'

'I have my godfather. And I've plenty of friends.'

'Menfriends?'

'And womenfriends,' she replied.

'You've never thought of marrying again?'

'The question has never arisen.'

'You mean you haven't met the right man?'

'Perhaps.'

His mouth stretched in a slow smile that caused a disarming dimple in his cheek. 'That,' he said, 'is a very cautious, very English reply, Mrs Blake. You're being reticent.'

'And you're being inquisitive,' she returned.

The smile widened into a grin. 'You mean I should mind my own business?'

Before she could reply, she saw Franz at the door. He came in, his expression carefully blank, and said something about clearing away the coffee things. Having gathered the cups and loaded the tray he added another comment, with a nod at the curtained window. *'Es schneit.'*

Snowing! Juli got to her feet, shaking out her whispering skirt before going to the window, which was set in an alcove, part of one of the towers of the castle. She pulled the tasselled blue drapes aside and knelt on the window-seat, though at first she could see little but the reflection of the room. Then the main lights went out behind her and she glanced round to see Franz with his hand on the switch.

Now the room was lit only by a standard lamp in a corner, and by the firelight. Outside she could see pine trees on a shoulder of hillside, where snowflakes fell thick and fast in the glow of one of the castle spotlights, and as her eyes adjusted she made out the twinkle of more lights far below, at the town in the valley.

She stared at the fairy-tale view, unaware that Andreas had moved until he said from right behind her, 'What do you see?'

His nearness disturbed her. Trying to ignore the unsteady leaps of her heart she said, 'Franz was right. It's snowing. There's a covering on the trees already.'

'It can be bad when it comes at this time of

year,' Andreas said, and his hand—perhaps by accident—brushed her back, only to pause as if surprised to meet bare flesh. After a second, he let his knuckles trail lightly across her shoulder-blade and when he spoke his voice had gone gruff. 'You're warm.'

'I've been sitting near the fire,' she said, glad to hear that she sounded calm even if her insides had turned to jelly. Was this a practised move—the manservant dimming the lights to create the right atmosphere for his master to make amorous advances?

'I miss so many pleasures,' Andreas murmured. 'I had no idea of what you were wearing, except that it whispers when you move.'

His fingers drew shivers from her nerve-ends as he slowly smoothed his palm along her shoulder. Disturbed beyond bearing, Juli twisted out of reach, turning to face him as she choked, 'Don't do that!'

'Why not?' he demanded, his face twisting suddenly, turned almost ugly with bitter scorn. 'Don't you like to be touched by a blind man?'

Juli caught her breath. 'That has nothing to do with it!'

'No?' he asked with a curl of his lip.

'No! Herr von Remmen, I . . . I don't know what kind of woman you're accustomed to meeting, but —'

'But you are not like them?' he broke in, mocking her. 'Ah, come, Mrs Blake, all women

44

are the same. Sisters under the skin—isn't that the saying? Doesn't it occur to you that I'm a rich man—that there might be generous rewards for your companionship?'

Suddenly Juli felt sick with disgust and disillusionment. She had let her own imagination betray her. Here was no prince from a fairy-tale; here was merely a worldly, cynical man to whom women were yet another commodity he might purchase. Taking a deep breath she said, 'If I chose to give a man my "companionship", Herr von Remmen, it would be because I wanted to—not for what I might gain. But you would probably never believe that. You'd always think I wanted something. Haven't you ever met a woman who wanted you for yourself?'

In the silence she heard the fire spit and crackle. Andreas's face bore no readable expression, though a muscle jumped in his jaw and Juli saw his hand clench and unclench at his side as if some fierce emotion stirred in him. 'You may go to bed, Mrs Blake. You have had a tiring day.'

Juli began to move away, all her sweet girlish dreams in shreds. 'Good night, Herr von Remmen,' she muttered.

*   *   *

After a restless night, Juli breakfasted with Madame Ghislaine. There was no sign of

45

either Sara or Andreas though Madame said her son was probably working in his study. Juli was not sorry; after the scene last night she hardly knew how she would face Andreas. Obviously he was nothing like the dream-image she had built in her mind.

When they had eaten, Madame took Juli on a conducted tour of the castle, showing her possible locations for the photographs which would be taken when the spring came. The big state rooms at Falkenruhe were almost overwhelming in their grandeur, used by the von Remmen business empire for conferences and meetings, and occasionally hired out to other companies. Juli's imagination was caught by ballrooms, grand halls, sweeping staircases . . . Already she was planning how she might arrange lighting and props.

Later, wearing a thick slate-blue sweater with grey slacks—all part of the mix-and-match set Howard had provided—Juli zipped up the warm jacket, wound the long scarf round her throat, snatched up a small camera and ventured outside to explore the castle grounds.

The snow had drifted on a swirling wind, so that in some places the ground was hardly covered while in others it lay inches deep, and it was still cold enough for the trees to retain their frosting of fluffy white on each branch and twig. Juli's breath misted the air in faint white puffs.

Following a path that curved up around the side of the castle, she discovered a garden backed by a rugged red cliff. Steps and pathways twined among a scatter of snow-clad trees, and one path climbed up under an archway of snowy branches at the side of the cliff. It led, apparently, to a ruin that was visible on the summit of the mountain.

Juli saw three people in the garden: a small boy dressed all in cherry-red was gleefully piling snow to make a snowman, encouraged by two well-wrapped women, one of whom Juli recognised as the young widow Sara von Remmen.

'Good morning!' Juli called.

The women looked round and Sara waved and called back a greeting before saying something to her companion and coming wading through ankle-deep snow towards Juli. Her red hair curled out from under a brown mink hat that matched her belted jacket, but no make-up enlivened her pale face or disguised the shadows under her eyes. Juli could not help but feel an empathy with the girl, whose situation was so like her own—except, of course, that Sara had her son. Little Karl must be a consolation to her.

'Finding your way about?' Sara asked, and sighed, pulling a face. 'Sorry about last night. I shouldn't drink so much wine. It always puts me straight to sleep. How did the evening go?'

'Oh . . . fine,' Juli said. 'None of us stayed up

very late.'

Sara huddled closer into her jacket. 'You seemed to be holding your own with Madame. Once or twice I thought she was going to choke.'

'I hope I wasn't rude.'

'You were a bit . . . forthright is the word, I think. I wish I had the nerve to answer her back, but she just makes me feel tongue-tied. She affects most people that way. Even Marie-Elizabeth daren't do much other than smile and nod and say 'Yes, Madame.'

Curious, Juli glanced to where the other young woman was now helping the small boy with the snowman. 'Marie-Elizabeth?'

Sara laughed aloud, bringing from the cliff a sharp echo that made her clap a gloved hand to her mouth. Over it, her green eyes gleamed. 'No, that's not her, that's Karl's nanny, Barbara Entwhistle—Nanny Bar, as he calls her. Marie-Elizabeth, on the other hand, used to be married to Andreas—and anybody less like Barbara Entwhistle you can't imagine. Marie-Elizabeth . . .' she rolled her eyes and tossed her head in an impression of hauteur, 'is related to Austrian royalty, my dear.' She grimaced, adding, 'Trouble was, she didn't have the funds to live in the style to which she wanted to become accustomed. Hence the von Remmen alliance.'

'That sounds like gossip,' Juli said, feeling uncomfortable about being the recipient of speculation into Andreas's private affairs.

'Oh, it's common knowledge,' Sara assured her. 'She married him for money. *He* married *her* because his mother fancied being related to a title. And then both of them went their own way—Marie-Elizabeth to the Riviera and the yacht set, Andreas to swing with the in-crowd in Paris, or Rome, or New York, or wherever . . . A real open marriage theirs was. Very modern. Very *avant garde.* That's how people like the von Remmens live. Didn't you know?'

Wondering why Sara sounded so cynical, Juli asked, 'Is that how it was with you and Heini?'

Sara hesitated, her green eyes troubled. Then she said, 'That was different. Heini loved me.' Her look darted defiance. 'He did!' she said as if she had been contradicted.

'I'm sure he did,' Juli replied gently.

'It didn't suit *them*, of course,' Sara went on. 'But they had to put up with it, because it was what Heini wanted. *I* was what Heini wanted. And now, because of that, I'm trapped here.' She glanced round as if fearing she might be overheard, then laid an urgent hand on Juli's arm. 'Mrs Blake . . . Can I talk to you? As a friend, I mean? I'm beginning to think I shall go mad if I don't talk to somebody.'

'Of course,' Juli replied at once, though she was disturbed by what Sara had said. Trapped here? Whatever did she mean?

'But we can't talk here. Not now. Andreas is on the prowl.' She nodded at the corner of the castle, where Juli saw Andreas standing with his head tilted as if listening, though probably all he could hear was Karl's merry yell as he tumbled in the snow.

'On the prowl?' she queried, thinking it an odd choice of words.

'Oh, don't let him fool you,' Sara said. 'He may not be able to see, but he doesn't miss a thing. He has his spies. We'll talk later. Maybe while Karl has his nap this afternoon.'

Another high-pitched shout came from Karl as he chased across the lawn, kicking up snow with his red boots. He was an elvish figure in padded jacket and trousers of bright red, with a red hat crammed down over dark, curling hair and his face glowing as he ran, calling, 'Uncle Andreas! Uncle Andreas!' He launched himself at the tall man, clutching his legs, and squealed as Andreas dropped the walking-stick he was holding and bent to swing his little nephew high in the air. Both of them were laughing as he held the child close and small arms hugged his neck as they talked to each other.

Juli discovered a lump in her throat. She had never thought of Andreas as a fond uncle. They made quite a picture, the child a splash of scarlet against the man's light-coloured jacket. Then she saw the resentment on Sara's face and guessed that the girl was thinking about her husband, wishing Heini were there instead of Andreas.

'Karl's lucky to have an uncle to turn to,' she commented. 'It's not the same, I know, but . . .'

'No, you don't know,' Sara broke in. 'You don't know at all, Mrs Blake. Excuse me.'

The nanny—a plain-faced girl in her twenties—crossed the lawn to relieve Andreas of the child. Sara joined them, but Karl objected to being removed from his uncle, or perhaps he objected to being take away from the snow. He was howling as his nanny conveyed him away.

Sara was about to follow when she was stopped by something Andreas said. He appeared to be enquiring about Juli's whereabouts; Sara answered him and half gestured at Juli before hurrying away. Andreas bent to retrieve the long walking-stick he had dropped, found it quite easily and straightened, his head turned in Juli's direction.

He was wearing a coat cut like a flying jacket, made of stone-coloured leather and lined with lambskin. A scarf, wrapped round his neck and folded inside the jacket's opening, echoed the pine green of his slacks, while his feet were encased in snow boots. Juli wondered whether Franz helped him choose what clothes to wear. Despite the cold, he was bare-headed, and in the bright snowlight his mirror-glasses didn't seem out of place.

'Julienne?' his voice came clear and almost commanding across the distance that separated them.

She hesitated, wishing she had been able to escape. She could still do so, but it would be unfair. 'Good morning, Herr von Remmen.'

She watched him walk with slow but firm steps towards her, using the stick to assess the lie of the land. Her heart twisted painfully as she recognised and applauded his courage. Another man might have let blindness be a handicap: Andreas had obviously taken it as a challenge to be met head on.

'I wish you would call me Andreas,' he said as he drew level with her. 'Or is that your way of reminding me to keep my distance?' He cocked his head, waiting for a reply. 'Julienne?'

In his mouth her name was composed of three distinct syllables, the 'J' slurred in the French way, so that it became 'Zhu-lee-enne.' No one else had ever pronounced it in quite that way and, despite herself, the sound sent quivers of pleasure up her spine.

'I'm here,' she said.

His head whipped round and she almost believed he was looking at her from behind those sunglasses; it gave her the weirdest prickly feeling, which hurt her, for his sake. 'Answer me when I speak to you!' he exclaimed.

'I would, if I had something to say!' she

returned in a tone that matched his for irritability. 'And who told you my first name?'

The question seemed to disconcert him and his frown bit deeper as he said, 'Howard Marston, I expect. Why? Do you object?'

'It just sounds odd,' she said lamely, regretting her edginess; it was too revealing. 'Nobody ever calls me Julienne any more. Especially not Howard. My name's Juli. Just Juli.'

'And I'm Andreas, not Herr von Remmen—not to you.'

Stuck for a reply, she blurted, 'Should you be out here on your own? Where's Franz?'

'You think I need a nanny, like Karl?' he demanded. 'I'm not alone—you're here with me. I thought we might take a walk. I'll show you the Falkenburg—the ruin up on the hill—if you'll be my guide.' He held out a crooked arm, but Juli didn't take it.

'Please?' he tried. 'Julienne . . . I want to apologise for the things I said last night. I was angry—with myself, not with you—but that's no excuse. I insulted you. And I'm sorry. Shall we—may we—pretend it didn't happen? Please!'

It was more an order than a plea, but Juli found her resistance wilting; his apology, at least, sounded totally sincere. 'It wasn't entirely your fault,' she said with a sigh. 'I'm sorry for the things I said, too.'

He was silent for a moment, frowning a

little behind the sun-glasses. Then he held out a gloved hand and said, 'Let us be friends, Julienne. Shall we walk? May I show you the view?'

Juli wondered if she was being naive and gullible again, but in this mood he was impossible to resist. Aware that he needed a guide, she gave him her hand. 'Yes, if you like,' she agreed.

They made for the path that climbed beside the cliff. Beneath the archway of snow-crusted branches steps had been cut from the soft red rock. Aware of the strong hand clasped firmly round hers, even through gloves, she found herself instinctively taking care of him, watching his feet so that he shouldn't stumble, and warning him when the branches grew so low that he might have knocked his head. They climbed slowly, talking about their surroundings.

He recounted the history of the Falkenburg—the medieval castle which down the centuries had figured in the political struggles of the Ardennes. Eventually it had fallen to ruin, perched there on its mountaintop as a relic of earlier days.

'Then in the eighteenth century a nobleman built the present Falkenruhe,' Andreas explained. 'People call it the Schlossel—the little castle, though in fact the original is probably the smaller, as you'll soon see.'

The tunnel of branches gave way to open

space, the rough path climbing on ahead to where Juli could now see the ruined walls of the Falkenburg, half hidden by trees and bushes under a covering of snow. But to her left the view spread in breathtaking depth, over a deep wooded river gorge.

'Explore on your own,' Andreas said. 'I'll only hold you back. No . . . it's all right, you go on. Just be careful.'

*   *   *

The ruin was romantic, tunnels of masonry, towering walls. Juli imagined it in springtime, gay with blossom and leaves unfolding, and with model girls wearing Howard Marston gowns whirling and posing against this background, with a light here, a reflector there . . .

Picking her way back to the path, she saw Andreas leaning against a gnarled tree, long legs braced and his dark head flung back as if to feel the sunlight on his face. Both hands rested on the carved head of the long walking-stick. How fine he looked—tall, strong, lean . . .

She paused to take a picture of him, to have another memento, foolish though she knew it to be. He attracted her irresistibly, as he had always done. If only . . .

She sighed to herself. 'If onlys' were for dreamers.

'Why are you sighing?' Andreas asked,

easing away from the tree. His hearing was uncannily sharp.

'Oh . . . no reason,' she lied. 'Just that it's so beautiful here. It's going to make a marvellous setting for fashion stills. What puzzles me is how Howard ever came to hear about it.'

'He saw an article about my mother that described Falkenruhe, so he said. And of course he knows of her involvement with the Chéri boutiques.' He smiled a little sardonically. 'Two birds with one stone—isn't that the expression?'

'Not very subtle, was he?' Juli had to agree.

'No, but mother was intrigued by the chance to meet him. And when you come in April with the model girls and the pretty clothes it will provide a diversion for Sara.'

'Is that why you agreed to the proposition— for Sara's sake?'

'In part. I won't pretend I shall enjoy having my privacy invaded, but perhaps I can arrange not to be here.'

Not be here? Juli thought, dismayed by the thought of returning in April and not finding him at Falkenruhe.

But he was saying, 'Julienne . . . I wanted to ask you, about Sara. You must have seen how dispirited she is. Is that a usual syndrome? Did it happen to you?'

In other circumstances Juli might have baulked at answering such a personal question, but he seemed genuinely concerned about

Sara. 'There was a time when there didn't seem to be any point in anything,' she admitted. 'I came through it eventually. Sara will, too.'

She recalled what Sara had said less than an hour ago. She had seemed frightened, but she must be lonely without Heini, and she probably found Falkenruhe, and Madame Ghislaine, overwhelming. She could be forgiven for letting her imagination run riot.

Andreas was listening with his head bent, his long fingers exploring the carving on the curved head of his stick. 'You must have been very young when you married.'

'I was nineteen. But I'd known Peter all my life. We grew up together. Getting married seemed the natural thing to do.'

'May I ask what happened?'

'He was a keen rock-climber,' she said quietly. 'There was a landslide. By the time they brought him down . . .'

Andreas let the silence lengthen before he said quietly. 'I'm sorry. It was a terrible thing for you.'

'Yes, it was.' Her voice had gone husky. She cleared her throat, shaking the memories away. Peter still had his place in her heart; that would never change. However, she no longer felt guilty because she was still alive and needed something more tangible than memories. 'But eventually I realised that the rest of my life was waiting. I was still young. I could still feel. I could even laugh. You must know how it is yourself. Didn't you feel the same, after your divorce?'

A grimace made a downward curve at one corner of his mouth. 'No, Julienne. I felt very little. There was nothing left between Marie-Elizabeth and me. We no longer cared enough even to hate each other. There was only indifference.'

'That's sad,' she murmured. 'I'm sorry.'

'And *I* am getting cold,' he said, offering her his arm. 'Shall we go back for lunch?'

The snow was beginning to melt as the sun climbed to its February zenith, its light glittering in drops that trembled on the edge of each twiglet. Beneath the tunnel of dripping branches the worn steps were wet and slightly slippery, but Andreas strode down them with a confidence that made Juli cling tightly to his arm.

Half-way down he stopped and smiled in her direction. 'I'm familiar with these steps. Don't concern yourself.'

As he spoke, a handful of snow from some branch overhead dislodged itself and fell, hitting his ear and scattering over his scarf. He said, *'Mensch!'* and dashed away the wet snow, unwinding his scarf and shaking it out, complaining that some ice had gone down his neck.

Juli tried to help, but he was making such a fuss that the incident took on a comical aspect.

Laughter bubbled out of her, which made Andreas pause and frown, though a smile was tugging at his mouth. He reached to the branches above his head, grasped one and shook it vigorously, dousing them both in more snow.

A shriek escaped Juli as a small melting iceberg showered over her. Then she saw that Andreas had ducked sideways and was teetering on the steps. With a cry of alarm she grabbed to save him.

'Andreas! Be careful! You'll fall!'

'Then hold me.' He threw his arms around her to envelop her in a suffocating bear hug as he bent his face to the soft silk of her hair. For a moment neither of them moved, then a shudder shook him and he gathered her closer, burying his face in the scarf at her throat.

For a moment she allowed herself to enjoy the sweetness of that embrace, then common sense forced her back to reality. 'Don't,' she managed, trying to push him away. 'Please don't.'

His arms tightened hurtfully for a second as he pressed his lips to the hollow below her ear. 'But I want to,' he said gruffly.

'But you mustn't!'

'Why not?'

'Please!' Juli begged again, disturbed by her own instinctive desire to respond. 'Don't do this to me, Andreas. You said—'

'I know what I said!' Raw agony sounded in

his voice and even through the thickness of winter clothing she felt the taut heat in him. *'Liebe Gott!'* he breathed, adding something she couldn't translate though the desperation of his tone troubled her.

Then suddenly he thrust her away from him and with little regard for his own safety went on down the steps. Terrified for him, she cried, 'Andreas!' and went after him, only to stop when she saw that by some miracle he was safely back on level ground and making for the castle.

She found herself shaking, not entirely from the cold. She didn't understand him, or herself. She only knew that what was happening between them was frightening, bewildering, overpowering in its intensity. And whatever it was, it was happening to both of them.

*   *   *

On her way down for lunch, Juli heard footsteps on the stairs behind her and saw young Karl thumping on the treads as he came rapidly down, with Sara not far behind calling, 'Karl! Come here!'

Giggling, the child came on, only to pause when he saw Juli in his way. Huge brown eyes gazed at her, still sparkling with mischief under the tumble of dark curls, but his hesitation gave Sara time to reach him and take firm hold of his hand.

'Naughty boy! You mustn't run away like that! You might have fallen down the stairs!' She glanced at Juli ruefully. 'Sorry about this. He's joining us for lunch. Can you stand it?'

'I'm sure I can,' Juli laughed, touching the child's glowing cheek. 'Hello, Karl. What a lovely boy you are.'

'He takes after his daddy,' Sara said. 'Heini was dark and good-looking, too.'

'Like Andreas,' Juli observed. 'It must run in the family.'

Sara looked blank. 'Andreas? Oh . . . yes, I suppose you're right. But then you know what they say—handsome is as handsome does. But we'd better go. Madame doesn't like being kept waiting.'

*   *   *

Young Karl's presence enlivened the lunch table, though his grandmother kept looking down her nose at his behaviour and Sara was on pins. But Andreas talked entertainingly with the child, making Karl's bright face light up beneath his cap of dark curls. Like his father the little boy might be, but he also bore a strong resemblance to his uncle. And Andreas adored him, that was evident. So why did Sara mistrust her brother-in-law?

Covertly, Juli watched Andreas, wondering what was going on in his mind. He had hardly

61

even acknowledged her presence and she felt on edge as she recalled their encounters both last night and today on the mountain. She wished she could make up her mind about him. He had turned out to be a complex man, not nearly as predictable as she had imagined. But one thing she was sure of—she didn't believe he was as devious and calculating as Sara seemed to think.

Andreas was smiling now, sharing a joke with his little nephew, but as Karl's shout of laughter rang round the room Madame Ghislaine snapped, 'Don't encourage him! We are at table! He should learn to behave properly! His manners are a disgrace!'

'He's only laughing!' Sara exclaimed.

Madame spitted her with a look like icicles. 'There is a time and a place for laughter. If he is to eat with us he should be quiet.'

Unfortunately, Karl's excitement turned into boisterousness and he jumped up on his chair, managing to catch the tablecloth and send a glass of wine spilling. He froze where he was, turning apprehensive eyes on his grandmother as she burst into a torrent of disapproval that was mostly aimed at Sara.

'Your fault! You've let him run wild! I always said you weren't fit to bring up a child. You haven't the first idea about discipline even for yourself!' She pressed a thin hand to her forehead, her rings catching the light. 'And now he has brought on one of my migraines!

You're so thoughtless, Sara.'

Sara was on her feet, her lips compressed and her green eyes bright with both anger and tears. She swept Karl up into her arms, said bitterly, 'I'm so sorry your grandson offends you,' and left the room, taking Karl with her.

Across the table, Madame's severe gaze met Juli's. 'I trust you'll excuse my daughter-in-law's manners, Mrs Blake. She is little more than a spoiled child herself.' She glanced aside as Andreas stood up, making his mother say, 'And where are you going?'

'I have some phone calls to make,' he said grimly. 'If you'll excuse me, *Maman*, Julienne . . .'

His departure made Madame Ghislaine blink and mutter more apologies, though Juli fancied the old woman's confidence was shaken. Andreas had clearly signalled his annoyance with her. After a few minutes, Madame excused herself, murmuring that she must lie down for an hour or two. Her migraine . . .

CHAPTER FOUR

It was snowing again, huge flakes like goosefeathers drifting down to whiten the mountain view as Juli stood at her bedroom window. She hoped the snow would not prevent her from leaving tomorrow. A retreat seemed in order, before something irrevocable happened. She had not come here to get involved.

A brisk knock on her door made her call, 'Come in,' thinking that Sara had arrived. Instead, the opening door revealed the tall, thin figure of Franz, who remained deferentially on the threshold.

'Mrs Blake . . . excuse me. Herr von Remmen asks if you will have coffee with him in his suite in the west tower. If it is convenient.'

Juli hesitated, her heartbeat accelerating disturbingly at the prospect of seeing Andreas again. But she had not forgotten her promise to meet Sara. 'Have you seen Frau von Remmen—the young Frau von Remmen? She did say she wanted to talk to me.'

'She will be with her son,' Franz said. 'If you wish, I will tell her you will see her later.'

'Oh . . . well, in that case . . . Thank you, Franz.'

He bowed slightly and gestured her to

64

follow him. 'I will show you the way, Mrs Blake. Please . . .'

The way proved to be not far, just along a corridor and up a short flight of stairs. Franz opened a door, said, 'Mrs Blake, sir,' smiled enigmatically at Juli and departed.

The room was a den, furnished for comfort and relaxation with deep armchairs and a huge curved settee in crimson leather on a thick-pile cream carpet. Bookshelves covered the lower walls, while above them hung a collection of antique guns, from a blunderbuss to a tiny derringer pistol.

Soft music floated from hidden speakers, a piece by Delius that formed a pleasant background in the cosy room, and Andreas stood by the fire that burned in a corner hearth. He was still wearing dark glasses but he had changed his clothes for grey slacks and a casual shirt of emerald velvet with the initials 'AvR' embroidered flamboyantly at the left breast.

Watching him, Juli was aware of a compelling attraction that drew her like a moth to the flame. Since the moment they met he had had that effect on her. But she must resist it.

'You wanted to see me?' she asked.

'Since my mother has taken to her room, and Sara is with Karl, it's my duty to entertain our guest. Do you like this music? Your English composers are so tuneful.'

'Yes, it's very pleasant,' she agreed. 'I also like Wagner, when I'm in the mood.'

'Ach, no!' he protested. 'Too heavy. Too much drama.'

'It's the drama I like—especially "The Flying Dutchman".'

'The lost soul, doomed to wander,' Andreas said with a rueful smile. 'Would you have sailed with him to save him?'

'I like to think so.'

His smile widened, doing strange, unwelcome things to her heart. 'You're a romantic.'

'I'm trying to cure myself of that,' she said crisply.

'You think it's a fault?'

Juli hesitated, wondering about it, then said, 'Not if you keep it under control.'

'Perhaps so. Myself, I rarely suffer from romantic delusions. I'm a realist. At least . . .' the pause was noticeable and she saw his brow furrow as he questioned his own statement, 'that's the image of myself I like to cultivate.' With the ease of familiarity, he moved to stand by the big curved settee. 'Will you sit down?'

'Thank you.' Ignoring the tacit invitation to join him on the settee, she chose one of the red leather armchairs, whose cushions gave under her with a sighing sound, making Andreas smile wryly.

'Are you avoiding me?'

'Let's say I'm being cautious.'

66

The thrust turned his smile rueful as he eased himself down onto the settee, lounging with an arm draped across the back. 'But of whom are you wary, Julienne? Of me, or of yourself?'

There was little point in her making excuses that both of them would know were lies. She said, 'Both, perhaps.'

'That's very honest,' he approved. 'Still, if I promise to behave like a gentleman, will you come and sit with me? I can't see you. I have only sound, and touch. Please . . .'

She could not deny such an appeal, especially when she herself wanted to be nearer to him. The chair whispered as she left it and Andreas held out his hand, saying, 'Tell me what you're wearing.'

'It's a dress,' she said, letting her fingers link with his as she stood before him. 'Rose-pink wool. Knitted top, crocheted sleeves and skirt . . .'

'Crocheted?' Apparently unfamiliar with the word, he put out his free hand, finding the curve of her hip and examining the lacy work of the skirt over its silk lining. Juli wondered if he knew that his touch made her tingle. She was beginning to feel light-headed. 'Ah—yes, I understand,' he said. 'It's pretty. Pink, you said? You were wearing pink last night. Do you like that colour?'

'On occasion. And how do you know I was wearing pink last . . .'

His smile was apologetic. 'Franz told me.'

'Oh,' Juli said, disconcerted to discover she had been the subject of discussion between the two. 'I see.'

As if on cue, a knock on the door heralded the arrival of the manservant bearing a tray of coffee with porcelain cups and silver pot. He placed it on a low table in front of the settee and discreetly withdrew.

Andreas tugged gently at Juli's right hand, drawing her down beside him and placing her hand flat on his knee. His long fingers explored the shape of her hand and paused at the dress ring she wore. 'What stone is this?'

'It's a topaz.' Unnerved by the warmth of his hands on hers, she found herself loquacious. 'It's supposed to match my eyes. At least, that's what Charles said when he gave it to me—Oh, Charles is my godfather. Sir Charles Blake. He became my guardian when my parents died, and later he also became my father-in-law. He still likes to keep an eye on me. I . . . I'm not sure he'd approve of my being here.'

'Here at Falkenruhe?'

'I meant in this room—in your cosy eyrie!'

Andreas lifted his head. He was very close to her, so that she could see her own twin reflections in the mirror-glasses she was starting to hate. She caught her breath as something caused a heightening of awareness between them. He laid his hand along her cheek, his thumb gently brushing her lips. All at once the room was an intimate place.

'I should very much like to know what you look like,' he said. 'May I?' and his free hand lifted to touch her hair.

Closing her eyes to shut out the sight of him so close, she steeled herself to bear the sweet torture of his touch.

'Your hair feels like silk,' he said in a husky undertone. 'Franz tells me it's fair. I know the colour now—a shade lighter than ripe corn. I can feel it. And your face . . .' He framed it in tender hands. 'Delicate, beautiful . . . Bear with me, please . . .'

She was trembling inside as she fought off the longing to be in his arms and know again the joy she had felt that night at Sharborough House. Crazy? Yes, but he was like a drug and she was addicted. It had been so long. So long!

With his fingertips he explored every feature, imprinting the shape of her face on his memory—her cheeks, her temples, her ears, her softly arched brows and closed eyes, and then her odd little uptilted nose. His fingers trembled lightly across her lips . . .

As if the words were being forced from him, he said gruffly, 'I want so much to kiss you. Julienne . . . Julienne . . .'

The warm hand against her cheek held her in place as he bent towards her and Juli found herself mesmerised as she had been that very first evening, caught in a spell only he could weave. When his lips met hers a spasm of delight moved through her, but as he began to deepen the kiss and draw her into his arms, threatening to swamp every shred of reason, panic made her pull free and hold him off.

'Please . . .' she managed. 'Please don't—'

'Do you still think we should get to know each other first?'

Quiet as the words were, they struck Juli with an almost physical force. He was quoting her own words back at her—words she had spoken to him that magical evening at Sharborough House. Seconds ticked by before she was able to draw breath enough to whisper, 'You remember?'

'How could I forget?' the answer came gruff and low. 'Miss Prim . . . in your neat grey gown. So afraid to break the rules and dance with a guest at the ball. I remember it very clearly.'

Juli felt as though a great weight had been lifted off her, but a pulse in her throat began to jump unnervingly, making her voice a croak as she confessed, 'I remember it, too.'

'I know you do.'

She stared at him, wishing she could read his expression. 'You *know*?'

A corner of his mouth quirked again in a little apologetic smile. 'Franz told me you recognised me when we met at the airport.'

Franz did. The thought made Juli feel uncomfortable. It had not occurred to her that the manservant might act as Andreas's spy. 'You mean . . . you've known since last night? Then why didn't you say something before now?'

'I'm not sure. Perhaps I thought it best to keep a few barriers between us. But today . . . today I find myself unable to be so strong. How can I deny fate? Ah—but I forgot—you do not believe in fate.'

Unsettled by the continued touch of his fingers against her cheek, she caught his wrist and drew his hand down, holding it between both her own. 'Do you remember every silly word I said that night?'

'Every word. Every gesture. Every expression on your face.'

His intensity disturbed her. 'That can't be true, Andreas. It was a magical interlude, but . . .'

'But we are both too sensible to believe it was anything more than the mood, the moment, the music . . . and the wine,' he ended for her.

'What else could it have been?' Juli said. 'Andreas . . . you must have been married at the time.'

'Yes.' He withdrew his hands from her, breaking all contact between them as he turned away and raked his fingers through his hair. 'Yes, you had every right to believe nothing good of me. Now please . . . will you pour the coffee?'

71

To be closer to the table, she slipped off the settee and knelt on the shaggy cream carpet, remembering that Andreas took his coffee black and without sugar. He sat with the cup between his hands, leaning forward on his knees while Juli watched him from her eye corner, wondering what was going through his mind.

In the quiet room the strains of Delius came lush and plaintive, rising to a climax. The record ended, the machine clicked to a stop. The ensuing silence was alive with nuances.

'I must apologise for my mother,' Andreas said at last. 'Sometimes her behaviour to Sara is unforgivable.'

Relieved at the switch to less personal topics, Juli defended her hostess. 'But she did have a migraine attack coming on. And Karl *was* a bit noisy. He's a darling, but he's a touch unruly, don't you think?'

'Perhaps so. Perhaps he is becoming spoiled. I want so much to make up to him for being without a father, and I'm concerned about Sara. She's lonely, and very unhappy.'

'But it's early days yet. Nine months isn't very long. Sara will recover, eventually. And Karl's too young to remember much.'

'I hope you're right,' he said, and the silence returned.

'Will you tell me something?' Juli ventured, aware that it was a sensitive subject, but she had to know. 'Your eyes . . . What happened?'

72

A heavy sigh escaped him and he drained his cup, pushing it on to the table before leaning back in the settee. He took off the dark glasses and rubbed his eyes as if they were aching, saying at last, 'There was an accident. Two years ago. The winter after you and I met at Sharborough House.'

'What sort of accident?'

'A very convenient one, so my wife must have thought.' He paused, his mouth twisting before he added, 'It gave her the excuse she needed to tell me she wanted her freedom.'

Juli stared at him in concern. 'You mean . . .' she managed, 'that's why she divorced you?'

'Let's say it was the last straw.'

'Andreas . . .' Hurting for him, she laid a hand on his knee without thinking and he immediately sat up, covering her hand with his, curling his fingers round to hold her there.

'When it happened,' he told her, 'we were in San Moritz. A winter holiday with friends. It was supposed to be a last attempt to save our marriage, but we both knew it was over between us. It had been over for a long time. We gave a party. There was a lot of wild talk, and bets made on the outcome of a race. Down the Cresta Run, you know it?'

'I've seen it on television,' Juli said, feeling chilled as she recalled the deadly corridor of solid ice down which men risked their lives and called it sport. 'You don't mean to say that you . . .'

73

'Why not? I'd done it before. And I was in the Olympic bob-sleigh team one year.'

'Were you?' she said in astonishment.

'Of course. In the four-man bob. Though that's different. The Cresta is singles, flat on the stomach, head first. Part of me wanted to make Marie-Elizabeth feel something for me again, if only fear. They told me she screamed when I crashed and went spinning off the track. I don't remember it. There was darkness. And when I woke up in hospital . . .' He opened his eyes, bleak grey pools in a face gone angular. 'More darkness.'

Juli found she was kneeling beside him with tears hot behind her eyes. 'Isn't there anything they can do?'

'No, nothing.' He stood up, almost pushing her aside as he moved a step or two away. 'If we're to be friends, you must accept that. I want no talk of miracles. I've seen too many doctors. There is no cure, Julienne. I'm blind. I must live with that. I must accept it. I *have* accepted it.'

'I know you have,' she said huskily, hurting for him. 'And I admire your courage. I'm not sure *I* could have taken it so well.'

He shook his head and turned back to face her. 'I haven't taken it well. Sometimes I rage against it. Self-pity is not very attractive.'

'It's not self-pity!' she denied, jumping to her feet. 'You'd be inhuman not to be angry at times. But you haven't given up, have you?

74

You still function pretty well.'

'I try,' he said, his smile appreciating her sturdy support. 'You're good for me, Mrs Blake. Do you have to go away tomorrow? Can't you stay—maybe a few more days?'

'No, I'm afraid I can't,' she breathed with regret. 'I have an assignment to complete. In the Bahamas. But we can keep in touch, if you like, and I'll be back with Howard in April and then . . . then we'll talk some more, and get to know each other some more. There's no hurry, Andreas, is there?'

He reached out a hand and she met it with her own. For a moment he held her hurtingly tight, then relaxed and drew her fingers to his lips, kissing them one by one, saying, 'No, Julienne, there's no hurry at all.'

*   *   *

Juli returned to her room, showered and half dressed in her underwear and a warm robe as she sat by the mirror and began her make-up for the evening. The brush paused as a soft tapping came at the door and Sara's voice called, 'Mrs Blake? Are you there?'

'Come in,' Juli called, watching the reflected door open and Sara appear wearing green velvet pants and a loose black top. But her eyes remained those of a lost and frightened child.

'You did say we could talk,' she reminded

Juli.

Juli swung round on the stool. 'Yes, of course we can. Do you mind if I carry on doing my face?'

'No, go ahead.' She sat on the end of the bed, watching Juli through the mirror. 'I've just been putting Karl to bed. He didn't have his afternoon nap. Got too excited at lunchtime. Really, Madame forgets he's only four years old. I'll bet Andreas and Heini weren't angels. But then they were probably confined to the nursery until they were old enough to be presentable in company.'

'Yes, probably so,' Juli agreed with a smile. 'Under strict control of their nanny, no doubt.'

'That's how Madame would like Karl to be,' Sara said. 'But I like to have him around. It's stupid that I'm not allowed to take care of him myself. I've nothing else to do with my time now I'm being forced to stay here.'

'Forced?' Juli queried.

Sara pulled a face. 'What else would you call it? Oh, I'm free to come and go, but when I mention leaving . . . that's when the portcullis clangs down. You don't know what it's like for me, Julienne.'

'It's Juli. Just Juli.' She filled a small brush with colour to shadow her eyes, while from behind her Sara commented,

'Andreas called you Julienne at lunchtime.'

Juli stared at her reflection, seeing her glowing complexion and bright eyes and wondering if they betrayed her feelings. Did Sara know that she had spent the afternoon with Andreas? 'Well, that is my name, but my friends call me Juli.'

'Oh, okay then—Juli it is.' Restless, Sara slid off the bed, wandering across to perch on the window-seat. 'I gather you're in the same boat as me. How long is it since your husband . . .'

'Five years this August,' Juli said, glancing round to face Sara squarely for a moment. 'Sara . . . I know it doesn't help when people say this, but . . . you *will* come through it.'

Sara stared at her unhappily. 'You're right— it doesn't help. Besides, that's not . . . I mean, I do miss Heini, but . . . well, there's more to it. I'm not sure I can explain. I wish you were staying longer. You're leaving in the morning, aren't you?'

'Weather permitting,' Juli said with a lightness that covered her real feelings. It was ironic—two days ago she had been annoyed with Howard for cajoling her into this trip; now she was dismayed at the thought of its ending so soon.

'But you'll be back again in April?' Sara asked.

'All being well, yes. Along with the models and the crew. You'll see just how unglamorous it all—'

A knock on the door interrupted her. She left her seat to answer it and found Franz outside, with a bottle of wine on a tray. His face was inscrutable, as ever. 'With Herr von Remmen's compliments.'

'Oh—thank you, Franz,' Juli replied, surprised but pleased by the hospitable gesture. 'Put it down on the table over there.'

He did so, bowed a little and departed.

In his wake, Sara bounded across the room to listen at the closed door for a moment or two before opening it and glancing out into the corridor, much to Juli's puzzlement.

'What are you doing?'

'That man!' Closing the door, Sara shuddered with revulsion. 'He gives me the creeps! He spies all the time.'

It was odd that Sara should express the same thought that had crossed Juli's mind earlier—that Franz behaved like a spy. Not that it necessarily meant anything sinister was going on. That was too melodramatic to believe.

'What is there to spy on?' Juli asked.

'Me!' Sara exclaimed. 'My movements. Who I talk to. Where I go. Not that there's anywhere to go, or anybody to talk to. Not here. That's why they brought me here. So they could keep an eye on me.'

Privately, Juli thought it considerate of Andreas and his mother to have taken Sara and Karl so much into their care. She had no doubt that they had done it out of family concern, though Sara was as yet in no mood to believe it. She was suffering from a touch of paranoia, believing that everyone was against her.

'Why don't you pour us both some wine?' she suggested, returning to the mirror and watching as Sara filled two glasses and brought one to stand it by her elbow, retreating to the window-seat with the other.

'Sara . . .' Juli ventured. 'How did you come to meet Heini?'

'In Switzerland. I was at finishing school there. Oh—don't say it—they didn't do a very good job on me, I know. I was always hopeless. I'm afraid I skipped a lot of classes—which is how I came to meet Heini, quite illicitly. The headmistress was furious. She threatened to have me expelled. Only by then it was too late.'

'Too late?' Juli queried.

Sara gave her a pale twitch of a smile. 'I was pregnant.'

'Oh. I'm sorry.'

'You needn't be. Karl's the best thing that ever happened to me. Whatever else I might wish to change, I'd never wish my baby unborn.'

Convinced of the sincerity of that declaration, Juli said, 'What about your parents? Where are they?'

'There's only my father. He . . . oh, he never was interested in me. After my mother died, he farmed me out with relatives, and at boarding-schools. I was just a nuisance to him.

79

He's married again now and his new wife doesn't want anything to do with me. They didn't even come to my wedding—they were on a lecture tour in the States. And after Heini died all I got was a letter saying the usual things. But between the lines it said they hoped I wasn't going to make demands on them.'

Juli looked round, pitying the girl. 'Oh, Sara . . .'

'I'm used to it,' Sara shrugged. 'Anyway, it means I can't turn to them, and who else is there? I've got nobody in the world that I can really talk to.'

'I do understand,' Juli said. 'I've been there myself. You know . . . Madame Ghislaine may not be an easy lady to feel close to, but she loved Heini, too. And so did Andreas. That's something you have in common. If you'd let them—'

She stopped in mid-sentence as Sara looked directly at her, green eyes cynical and bleak. 'They don't care about me. I was never good enough for them. Not up to von Remmen standards.'

Taken aback, Juli said, 'I'm sure that's not true, Sara.'

'Of course it's true! Oh, you don't understand, Juli. I knew you wouldn't. You've only seen their pleasant social side. They want to impress you.'

'They're also concerned about you. I know

that from what Andreas has said. He knows you're not happy. It bothers him a lot.'

Sara curled her feet under her, looking doubtful. 'Does it? I wonder.' She took a long drink, nearly emptying her glass. 'Has he told you I'm overwrought? That's what he calls it. I'm overwrought, so I have to be protected from myself. I'm overwrought, so I can't be allowed to stay in the flat in the city, where I was happy. And I can't be trusted to look after Karl. I'm overwrought—so nobody believes a word I say.'

'Andreas hasn't said anything of the kind,' Juli denied.

'No? Well, don't worry, he will—especially when he finds out we've had this chat. And he will find out. Franz will tell him. And then dear brother-in-law Andreas will be anxious to explain to you how I imagine things. I've not been well, you know. That's what he'll say.'

'Well, isn't it the truth?'

'I was upset, not sick! They had no call to send for a doctor. He put me on tranquillisers, to turn me into an obedient zombie—all for my own good, of course.'

Her bitterness troubled Juli. 'Sara . . . losing someone you love can be devastating—mentally and physically. *My* doctor prescribed medication to help me over the worst when Peter died. There's nothing sinister about that.'

'Oh, I'm not saying they wish me harm,'

Sara said. 'But all they really care about is Karl. Karl is the heir to all this,' a gesture encompassed the castle and its surroundings, 'and so he has to live here, under von Remmen control. I've got two choices, you see—I stay here with Karl, or I go away—without him.'

Convinced that the girl was exaggerating, Juli said, 'They wouldn't expect that of you. You're Karl's mother.'

'But his father was a von Remmen!' Sara cried, leaping up to pace the carpet in agitation. 'How can I fight them? They'd bring all the top lawyers in the country to plead their case. And they'd win. They'd make sure of that. Karl's their only hope for the future.'

'But surely . . .' Juli reasoned, 'Andreas is still young enough to have a family of his own. He might produce half a dozen other heirs. It's a little early to—'

Sara stopped pacing and flung out her arms. 'That's just the point! Andreas won't have any children. He has no intention of ever getting married again.'

This news made Juli's mind go momentarily blank with shock. 'Is that what he said?'

'He *means* it. Marie-Elizabeth led him quite a dance, you know. Then she walked out on him when he most needed her moral support, *and* she took him for all she could get when they were divorced. It put him off marriage for good, so he won't be fathering any other little von Remmens, will he? Karl is all they've got,

82

and they're not going to let him out of their sight. And *I'm* not going anywhere without him. *Now* do you understand why I feel trapped here?'

Feeling numb, Juli slipped out of her wrap and put on the HM version of the classic 'little black dress', of clinging jersey crepe with a spiral of gold drops. But she wasn't thinking about the dress, or of anything but Sara's claim that Andreas would never marry again.

It couldn't be true. It must be something he had said in a moment of bitterness.

'You think I'm hysterical, don't you?' Sara sighed. 'You don't believe me.'

'I believe you're unhappy,' Juli said. 'Because of that, you're not seeing things in their proper perspective. Give it time, Sara. You have a lovely home, people who care about you, and a little boy who needs you. The rest will sort itself out, believe me.'

Pushing back a stray red curl that was falling over her eyes, Sara sighed heavily. 'Maybe you're right, Juli. It's helped me just to talk. Would you like to come with me to see if Karl's okay? Then we'll go down to dinner.'

*   *   *

A nightlight in the shape of a friendly dwarf stood on a bedside table, its glow falling across the single bed where four-year-old Karl von Remmen lay sleeping. His dark hair was fluffy from his bath and long dark lashes swept across his plump cheeks as his mother pulled the duvet more closely round him and bent to drop a kiss on his curls.

'He's beautiful,' Juli whispered, and a soft smile lit Sara's face as she glanced round.

'I think so, too, of course. He looks so sweet when he's . . .' Her eyes flicked past Juli, the smile died, and all at once she looked haunted again. The cause of the change was a slight girl in a grey dress and apron—Barbara Entwhistle, the nanny—who had appeared from nowhere as if in answer to some threat to her young charge.

'I didn't come to disturb him!' Sara breathed. 'I wanted Mrs Blake to see him. Something wrong with that?'

The nanny's plain face was expressionless as she replied in a flat, northern-English accent, 'No, of course not, madam,' and opened the door wider, inviting Sara and Juli to leave.

Sara grasped Juli's hand and led her out to the corridor, hustling her away and down a flight of stairs to another passageway, where she paused and turned, a tear glinting on her cheek. 'You see how it is. I can't even go near him without someone checking on me. Do they think I'm going to harm my own son?'

'But he was asleep,' Juli said. 'She didn't mean—'

'Of course she meant it! Oh . . . why should you believe me? No one ever believes me!' She broke away, fending off Juli's attempts to stop her. 'No, leave me. I'm not hungry. Tell them . . . tell them I've got a headache and want an early night. *Please*, Juli! If you're my friend, make up some excuse for me. I really don't think I can face them.'

CHAPTER FIVE

Madame Ghislaine was evidently still feeling the after-effects of her migraine. She was beautifully dressed and made-up, but her eyes had that tired, faded look that told of her drained energy. Beside her chair, Andreas stood as he had the previous night, wearing his dark glasses, his head tilted as he listened to Juli's explanation of Sara's absence.

'Hah!' Madame snorted. 'I, too, do not feel one hundred per cent well, but I have made an effort. You must forgive Sara, Mrs Blake. She has no manners.'

'She's under a strain,' Andreas said.

His mother sent him a snapping glance, her mouth set. 'Always you make excuses for her, Andreas. The truth is, she is selfish. But . . .' Forcing a smile,' she turned back to Juli. 'We shall not display our family squabbles in front of our visitor. How delightful you look, Mrs Blake. Another of Howard Marston's designs? He's a clever man—and not only with fabrics. He chose the perfect ambassadress.'

Madame was all graciousness over dinner, despite the lack of appetite following her migraine. She engaged Juli in polite conversation, interrupted from time to time by dry remarks from Andreas that eventually made his mother say sharply, 'Be serious,

Andreas! I'm in no mood for your jokes!'

He was instantly solicitous. 'Forgive me, *Maman*. Is your head still troubling you? I'm sure Mrs Blake would understand if you wish to go to your room and rest.'

'I shall go after dinner, thank you. No doubt Mrs Blake, too, will need an early night if she is flying back to London tomorrow. The weather is changing. They predict the snow will all be gone by the morning, so there should be no problem getting to the airport.'

'I'm sure Mrs Blake is relieved to hear it,' Andreas said lightly. 'She is a busy lady. By the end of next week she plans to be in the sunshine of the tropics, so she tells me.'

Madame's eyes widened with curiosity and interest. 'The tropics?'

'The Bahamas,' Juli explained. 'For a travel feature. But . . .' she glanced at Andreas, wondering why he had reminded her that she would soon be thousands of miles away, 'my stay has been most enjoyable, Madame. I shall look forward to coming back in six weeks' time.'

'As we shall look forward to renewing the acquaintance,' came the smiling reply as Madame dabbed her lips on a napkin and rose to her feet. 'So . . . shall we take coffee in the sitting-room?'

*   *   *

It had been almost a repeat of the previous evening; Madame had poured coffee, drunk one small cup and taken her leave. Now once again Juli was alone with Andreas, with the fire crackling and the room pooled by lamplight.

She stood by the fireplace, watching him as he sat on the pagoda-printed settee, remote behind those horrible glasses. 'Would you like some more coffee?'

'No, thank you.' He held out his hand. 'What I would most like is to have you near me, Julienne. If we are not to be snow-bound, we must make the most of the few hours we have left.'

Slowly, she reached to meet his hand, feeling his fingers catch and twine with hers as he drew her down beside him.

'What's wrong?' he asked.

'Nothing's wrong.'

'Don't lie to me. You've been quiet since you came down to dinner. What's troubling you?'

She stared at the leaping flames in the fire. 'I keep thinking about Sara. You're right to be concerned about her, Andreas. She seems to think the whole world's against her.'

'Particularly me—and my mother,' he sighed. 'Yes, I know. To hear her talk, you would think we were monsters.'

Juli lifted her head to look at him. 'She said she's being forced to stay here.'

'And did you believe her?' he asked.

'The thing is that *she* believes it! She's all mixed up. She seems to think she's in danger of losing Karl. Which is crazy. Isn't it?'

'*Liebchen* . . .' He curled his arm around her shoulders. 'Sara is young and—forgive me, but it's true—she is not very intelligent. She reacts with her emotions rather than with her head, and at present her emotions are not to be trusted. She is overwrought.'

Overwrought—she wished he hadn't used that word; it was just what Sara had predicted he would say. But that didn't make it any less true. Whatever one called it, Sara was in no state to think clearly.

'I, too, am sorry for her,' Andreas was saying. 'But she is not yet ready to go back to her apartment in the city, certainly not with Karl. As head of the family, I'm responsible for Karl's welfare. Until I'm sure that Sara can protect her son properly, I shall keep him here—under my protection. If the places had been reversed, I would have expected Heini to do the same for me.'

That sounded reasonable, Juli thought. Of course he wanted to protect his little nephew. Andreas would protect all his family if he felt it necessary. He was that sort of man. Sara was wrong about his ulterior motives. Entirely wrong!

'But you have no children of your own,' she commented.

'No.'

'Was that from choice?'

Momentarily, his arm tightened round her as if her questions disturbed him, then he said, 'At first we decided to wait a year or two, and later . . . later neither of us wished to involve children when we both knew our marriage was a disaster. The last few years we hardly saw each other. We remained married only because there was no urgent reason for seeking a divorce.'

Juli looked up at him. 'So when you and I met, you were separated from Marie-Elizabeth?'

'We had lived our separate lives for some while before that.'

He couldn't possibly know what a burden that lifted from her mind. 'But this afternoon you said you went to San Moritz in a last attempt to save your marriage.'

'Yes. I thought we should give it one final try. But it was futile. Even if the accident had not happened, it would not have worked out. As it was . . . she always hated illness of any kind.'

'She hurt you, didn't she?' she guessed. 'Is it because of her . . .' She hadn't meant to ask but the words came rushing out, 'is that why you said you'd never marry again?'

She waited breathlessly for his answer. At last, he took a deep breath and said, 'Who told you that?'

'Sara did. Is it true?'

'Yes,' he replied, his voice deep and definite. 'Yes, it's true. I shall remain single. I prefer it that way.'

Juli sat up, clutching at his hand, letting her gaze run over his dark hair and the strong, beautiful face half hidden behind those awful mirror glasses.

'That's crazy!' she breathed. 'I don't believe you mean that. Just because one woman hurt you . . . Andreas, you can't intend to waste your life. You have so much to give. You're an attractive man. You're warm, caring . . . You weren't made to be alone. Whatever Marie-Elizabeth said, or did, she's just one woman. You could find someone else—someone who would make you happy.'

His smile held more pain than amusement. 'Someone like you, you mean?'

She hesitated, unwilling to admit that she had been casting herself in the role. 'I wasn't thinking of anyone in particular. I just don't believe anyone can choose to stop having feelings. I always thought there'd never be anyone but Peter, but lately I've begun to see that it's not necessarily true. You withdraw, after you've been hurt, but you can't shut yourself off for ever.'

'You almost make me believe it's true,' he said, drawing her closer. 'We'll talk of this again, *Liebchen*. When April comes.'

The following morning, Juli left Falkenruhe as she had arrived—in the Mercedes chauffeured by Franz, with Andreas von Remmen beside her. But this time he was close beside her, warmly companionable, and Juli knew that he was as reluctant to let her go as she was to leave him. His hand around hers was at times painfully tight.

They were still holding hands as they stood on the concourse at the airport, waiting for the final call for her flight to London. Crowds of people moved to and fro around them and Franz hovered at a discreet distance, but Juli was aware only of the tall man by her side, and of the sadness that lay heavy on her heart.

'April seems like a year away,' she said. 'Stupid, isn't it?'

'The Bahamas might help,' he replied, smiling a tight smile. 'All those bronzed and muscular young men vying for your attention. You'll forget me.'

She looked up at him, wishing he didn't feel obliged to wear those horrible glasses. They were intended to alert strangers to the fact of his disability, but they also served to hide most of his expression. Right at this minute she would have given much to know what he was thinking.

'Why do you keep saying things like that? Is that what you want? That I should go away and forget you? Andreas . . .'

Over the public announcement system came mellow female tones announcing the last call for the flight to London. It rang in Juli's ears like the voice of doom as she watched Andreas's face for what seemed like eons of unbreathing. Surely he was going to reassure her, tell her that he wanted her back? She clung to his hand, willing him to say something, unable to believe he could remain silent.

Then he said gruffly, 'That was your flight being called. Better hurry or you'll miss it. Goodbye, *Liebchen*.' Cupping her face in his hands, he bent to kiss her with bruising passion. A moment later he spun on his heel, snapped, 'Franz!' and began to walk away, leaving her staring after him with wide, tear-bright eyes.

As the plane lifted off she glimpsed the spectacular ravines that split Luxembourg City, but they were dazzling and indistinct through the mist in her eyes. Juli felt as though her head might explode with grief. What had that leave-taking meant? Why hadn't Andreas given her something to hold on to—some word of affection, some sign that he wanted her to come back? Or had she been deluding herself to think he might care for her?

*   *   *

In some ways the rush to be ready for her working-trip to the Bahamas proved to be a blessing—it gave her an excuse to evade too many questions about her two days in Luxembourg.

'It snowed most of the time,' she told Charles. 'But it's a really beautiful country. Have you ever been there?'

'Passed through it once, I seem to remember,' her godfather replied. 'Give me London any day.'

This typical reply made Juli laugh. 'Honestly, Charles! You're a terrible old chauvinist. You dislike anything that isn't British.'

'Something wrong with being patriotic?' Charles asked.

'No, but it shouldn't stop you from seeing that other countries have their charm, too— lovely scenery, nice people . . .'

'Like whom?' he queried mildly enough, though his dark eyes were suddenly watchful and inquisitive. 'No one in particular!' she exclaimed, hoping her flush wasn't too evident. 'Everyone I met was charming. You'd have liked Madame Ghislaine. Maybe I should arrange a meeting between the two of you.'

Which made Charles humph and redden and deny having the least interest in women— not at his age, not any more.

*   *   *

94

To Howard, over dinner at an Italian restaurant one evening, Juli spoke mostly of Madame Ghislaine.

'She seemed really impressed with your designs. It was a good idea to let me take some outfits to wear. She said to tell you she's looking forward to meeting you. And the castle is going to make a marvellous background. I've taken some snaps to show you what it's like. It's all set for April.'

'You got on well with the old girl, didn't you?' Howard asked, blue eyes shining. 'I knew you'd do a good job for me, Jules.'

'I did my best. But I wouldn't think of her as an "old girl", if I were you, Howard. She's still very much a force to be reckoned with.'

'And her son?'

Juli became busy with her *moules marinières*. 'I don't think he has much to do with the boutiques. He runs the industrial side.'

'That wasn't what I meant,' Howard said. 'What's he like?'

'He's bright.' She glanced up, throwing up a smoke screen by laughing at him. 'You didn't fool him for a minute. He knows you're angling to sell your clothes to "Chéri". But as a canny businessman himself he seemed to approve of your nerve.'

'And did he approve of my designs?'

Her smile died. Suddenly her heart was

aching for Andreas. She missed him badly. 'He couldn't, Howard. He lost his sight in an accident two years ago.'

Howard stared at her. 'I'd no idea.'

'No, how could you? I didn't know it, either, not at first. He covered it so well. He must have immense courage to have coped with it the way he does. He still runs the von Remmen business empire, he travels . . .' She stopped herself, realising that she would give herself away if she went on. Andreas was so much on her mind that she wanted to talk about him constantly. 'Anyway, he's quite happy with the idea of our going back for the picture session. All you have to do is work on charming his mother. That's one formidable lady. But you don't usually have much trouble with women, as I recall.'

'Except where you're concerned,' Howard said mournfully. 'With you I have nothing else but trouble.'

Not wanting to get into an argument on that subject, Juli said, 'You haven't told me how the gala went. Was it an enormous success?'

Howard was only too ready to talk about the charity show and his meeting with the Princess of Wales. It had been a personal triumph.

After the meal, he drove her home to the converted Thames-side warehouse where her flat lay on the top floor, and wished her a safe trip to the Caribbean. 'No doubt you'll come back all tanned and delectable. Wish I were going with you.' He gazed at her with mournful blue eyes. 'Have I ever told you how empty London feels when you're not here?'

'Frequently,' she laughed. 'And I don't believe a word of it.'

'That's just the tragedy,' Howard said, and leaned to kiss her as he usually did at the end of a date.

Juli turned her cheek, only realising the significance of the gesture when she felt Howard hesitate in surprise. After a moment he brushed his lips across her cheek and drew back to give her a searching look.

She smiled at him, said, 'Thanks for the dinner. Good night, Howard,' and let herself through the door into a lobby where she stood for a moment examining the way she was feeling. Her affection for Howard hadn't changed, but she knew now that it would never be anything more. She knew that for sure because now she had found the right man— the only man she wanted to kiss and hold and be with. And his name was Andreas von Remmen.

*   *   *

The journalist with whom she was working in the Bahamas was a laconic middle-aged man named Jerry South. While working he was single-minded, but after hours when they relaxed together over a drink he revealed a preoccupation with the problems he and his wife were encountering with their teenage children. Many times, remarks he made reminded Juli of Sara von Remmen and her misunderstandings with Andreas and Madame Ghislaine.

Not that she needed much reminding of all that had happened at Falkenruhe. The memories went with her everywhere. Sitting in the shade of palm trees, drinking daiquiris with Jerry, she would find herself mentally back on the snowy mountain, by the fire in the blue sitting-room, or warm in the private tower apartments of the castle. With Andreas.

She couldn't wait for April to come.

*   *   *

She arrived back in England with a glowing tan and on reaching her flat dropped everything to grab up the mail that had arrived in her absence. She flipped through the envelopes, looking for Air Mail logos, or Luxembourg stamps . . .

But of course Andreas probably didn't write letters other than business ones through a secretary. Eagerly Juli listened to the tapes on her telephone answering-machine. Messages there were, but none from Andreas. Still, she assured herself, he had known she would be away. There had been no point in his contacting an empty flat.

She soon discovered that plans for the photo trip to Luxembourg were well advanced. Howard had made most of the arrangements and had booked the services of three models. When Juli called round at his workrooms, which as usual were in a state of organised chaos with humming sewing-machines and racks of dresses covered in polythene, Howard told her that most of the crew were to be accommodated at a Gasthof in the village below Falkenruhe.

'But you and I are to be guests at the castle. Along with . . .' he paused for dramatic effect, his face alight. 'You'll never guess.'

'So tell me,' Juli said, in no mood for games.

'Lyana! She's actually going to be available to model for us.'

Juli felt as though she had been kicked somewhere around the solar plexus. For a moment she couldn't get her breath. 'Lyana?'

'Yes.' He widened his eyes at her, mocking her apparent ignorance. 'You know—the model—the internationally famous Eurasian—'

'Howard, I do know who Lyana is!' she interrupted tartly. 'I'm just surprised to hear she'll be at Falkenruhe.'

'I gather she's doing it as a personal favour to Madame Ghislaine—apparently it was Madame who discovered her in Hong Kong and got her a start in the business. Lyana often stays at Falkenruhe. She's a friend of the family.'

'Really.' That was news to Juli, whose mind went back to the Edwardian Ball at Sharborough House, when the lovely young model in her silks and feathers had made such a perfect foil for Andreas's lean elegance. He had said he was escorting her as a favour to his mother. Could that have been no less than the truth, however unlikely? Juli wanted to believe it.

On the other hand, she was female enough to entertain doubts. If the beautiful Lyana often stayed at Falkenruhe when Andreas was there . . . Annoyed with herself, she cut the thought off short.

Howard was watching her shrewdly, knowing her too well to be deceived. 'Something wrong with that?'

'No, nothing at all,' she lied, avoiding his eyes. 'Any other surprises?'

'None that I can think of.' But his voice had gone thoughtful. Taking her arm, he drew her into his private office and closed the door. 'Are you all right? You seem very edgy.'

'I'm keyed up. Aren't we all? This trip could be important. Look, Howard, I really have to go. I've got a busy day ahead. So unless there's anything else . . .'

He let her go, but she guessed she hadn't heard the last of it. Howard sensed there was something wrong. But how could she tell him that she felt restless, lost, like a spare part in her own life because she had heard nothing from Andreas von Remmen?

*   *   *

On the day before the Luxembourg trip, Sir Charles Blake treated Juli to lunch and afterwards drove her home. Spring sunlight sparkled on the river and a cruiser went by laden with early tourists; the trees were unfurling new leaves, busy with fledglings trying their wings, but Juli's nerves were still at full stretch. She was looking forward to going back to Falkenruhe, yet at the same time she was dreading it. And she knew that Charles, like Howard, was aware of her mood if not of the cause of it.

'What a beautiful day it is,' he remarked as they climbed from the car and stood for a moment watching the traffic on the river. 'Let's hope the weather lasts for you.'

'Yes,' Juli said.

Charles glanced at her from his eye corner and put on a smile. 'Springtime in Luxembourg. Should be romantic. If I were in Howard's shoes . . .'

'Oh, don't, Charles, please!' she sighed. 'Do you realise you've spent the last two hours telling me what a splendid fellow Howard is?'

'Well, it's true!' He widened his eyes under bushy brows, the picture of innocence. 'He is a splendid fellow.'

'I know,' she sighed.

101

'So why aren't you looking forward to spending some time with him?' her godfather asked. Head on one side, he laid a hand on her shoulder and looked into her eyes. 'Darling girl, Howard is very, very fond of you. But no man's going to wait for ever. If you miss this chance, there might not be another.'

He was right, she knew. She might be happy with Howard, but . . .

Before she could find an answer, a motorbike came roaring along the riverside, its rider in the uniform of one of the city delivery services. He stopped behind Charles's car and extracted a package from his pannier, striding with it to ring Juli's bell. Intrigued, she crossed the paving, saying, 'Is that for me?'

'Mrs Blake?' the youth enquired. 'Sign here, please.'

Juli did so and as the messenger departed she examined the flat, oblong parcel.

'Special delivery?' Charles said, peering over her shoulder. 'How exciting. Expecting something, are you?'

'No, nothing. I can't imagine what . . .' Overcome by curiosity, she tore off the wrapping and paused at sight of a velvet-covered jewel case. What was this—something from Howard, or a going-away gift from Charles? But her godfather seemed as mystified as she was.

'Well, open it,' he urged.

Suddenly fumbling, Juli unclipped the clasp

of the flat box and opened the lid, disclosing a piece of folded notepaper lying on top of a beautiful antique necklace of topazes set in intricate filigree silver. She picked up the note holding it safe between fingers and thumb as she showed Charles the necklace. She was too choked with emotion to speak. The necklace was the loveliest thing she had seen.

'Ha!' Charles exclaimed. 'That'll match that ring I gave you. Good for Howard. He's got more imagination than I gave him credit for. It is from Howard, is it? What does he say?'

Some instinct warned her that the gift might not be from Howard—it was not Howard's style to do things this way. She put the note, unread, back in the box and closed the lid, saying, 'I'll read it when I get inside. Charles . . . please excuse me, but I've got a million things to do. Thanks for lunch. I'll see you when we get back from Luxembourg, okay?' Not daring to meet his eyes, she brushed a swift kiss across his cheek and escaped, glad when the outer door closed behind her and she could run up the stairs to the privacy of her flat.

*　　　*　　　*

The necklace of topazes and antique silver was just as lovely on second sight, but Juli's hands were shaking as she opened the piece of paper. Scrawled across it were the words, 'Forgive me—Andreas.'

Forgive him? she thought with a quirk of disquiet. Oh—he meant because he hadn't been in touch before, that must be it. But he had been busy. She understood that. It was enough that he had contacted her now. Tomorrow . . . tomorrow she would see him again.

Tears of joy bit behind her eyes. In an ecstasy of delight she kissed the note he had written with his own hands. He had sent the necklace to assure her he was waiting. He had tried to stay aloof, but he couldn't. Oh, now she could look forward to seeing him again. All at once the spring sunlight was full of promise.

And then, taking a closer look at the notepaper he had used, she realised it was headed 'Savoy Hotel, London.' Andreas was here in England! She needn't wait even one day to see him.

She grabbed for her phone and with trembling fingers dialled the hotel's number, waiting for what seemed an age before a receptionist answered and she was able to ask for Herr von Remmen's suite.

'I'm afraid Herr von Remmen checked out a couple of hours ago,' the receptionist replied.

Juli didn't believe it. 'He can't have done! A couple of hours? How long did he stay with you?'

'Let me see . . . ah, yes, he was here for six days.'

Six days! Juli felt stunned. If Andreas had

been in London for six whole days, why hadn't he called her? 'Where was he going?' she asked. 'Did he say if he was returning home to Luxembourg?'

'They were going to Heathrow, catching a flight to the States,' the girl informed her helpfully. 'His valet said something about a business conference. I'm afraid they didn't leave any forwarding address.'

Juli never remembered putting down the phone. 'His valet' was Franz, presumably. Oh, yes, Franz would be in on this without a doubt. A business conference, was it? No wonder Andreas asked to be forgiven! The necklace was a goodbye gift.

He wouldn't be at Falkenruhe.

Well! Juli thought with brittle, bitter humour, that should teach her a lesson. She ought to have known it was hopeless, right from the start—right from that first evening at Sharborough House when she had stupidly let him enchant her.

So okay. It was all over. So what? There were other men in the world.

She started to pack, throwing things into a suitcase in wild disorder, but her thoughts went racing on, bitter, hurt, angry, until she couldn't bear it any more and she sat down on her bed, head in hands as pain raged through her and sobs wrenched her whole body. She had been a fool. But, oh, it had been such a lovely dream!

CHAPTER SIX

Luxembourg was as lovely in April as Juli had always imagined it would be. The forested hills of the Ardennes were alive with birdsong; the valleys and rugged river gorges burgeoned with green leaves and spring blossom. At Falkenruhe the fountain in the lower courtyard was flowing again, and the great tubs that decorated the steps were planted with spring flowers. It was beautiful. Juli could see that with her eyes, but she couldn't feel it with her heart. Falkenruhe, without Andreas, might as well have been a desert.

'Andreas found it necessary to deal personally with some business in New York,' Madame Ghislaine explained. 'We don't expect him back for two or three weeks. I'm sure he will be sorry that he missed seeing you.'

'Oh, not at all,' Juli replied with one of her brightest smiles. 'We didn't expect him to be here in person. Did we Howard?'

Howard and Madame Ghislaine had taken to each other on sight and could be found talking endlessly about trends in fashion, often with Lyana nearby. Lyana, Juli had discovered, was not only beautiful, she had the sweetest disposition. Despite herself, Juli could not help liking the lovely Eurasian.

The other two models were having a great time, along with their dressers, and the make-up girl, and a couple of young men Howard had commandeered from his staff to drive the minibus and help move heavy equipment like Juli's photographic lights. The crew worked hard, but their off-duty time was fun, sightseeing, or down at the local beer cellar. They were happy not to be at the castle; they found Madame Ghislaine a little overpowering.

Juli worked hard, too, though she worked mechanically, placing her lights just so for the right effect and getting the models to move, pose, smile and pout. She found Lyana an instinctive subject who hardly needed instruction. And there was young Karl, called in to add interest to some of the shots while his nanny hovered not far away and Sara watched with bright eyes.

Seeing Sara drawn out of herself by all the activity was one of Juli's main consolations, especially since it was just what Andreas had hoped for. Sara laughed a lot, and flirted gaily with Howard, who flirted right back. It was, Juli thought, probably the best medicine Sara could have had.

At the end of another tiring day—a day when inclement weather had made them decide on indoor shots—the crew were in the Grand Ballroom. Outside, April rain dripped down from a grey sky, making the huge room gloomy now that the photo-floods had been switched off. Voices echoed and footsteps shuffled as the models changed behind a screen and the men shifted lights and reorganised furniture—with 'help' from young Karl—while Juli knelt in a corner to pack her cameras and lenses in their case. Not far away, Howard was advising Sara on the style she ought to adopt to bring out her best features. He visualised her as ravishing in hats.

'I look like a prune in a hat!' Sara laughed.

'No, you won't,' said Howard. 'Especially if it's veiled. Very Mata Hari. Don't you think so, Jules?'

Juli looked up, putting on the smile she wore like a mask. 'I always rely on your judgement, Howard.'

'Hats! Me!' Giggling, Sara turned to Juli, saying, 'Aren't you going to have an hour or two free before you go back to England, Juli? I've been hoping to have a chance to show you the country.'

'Does that invitation include me?' Howard wanted to know.

'No, certainly not!' Sara chaffed, waving him away. 'No men allowed. I want to talk to Juli in private. Girl-to-girl stuff. What do you say, Juli?'

Carefully packing her fish-eye lens, Juli said, 'You'll have to ask my boss.'

'Oh, go ahead,' Howard agreed affably. 'I expect I can find some way of amusing myself for an afternoon.'

'Great!' Sara enthused. 'I did think we might take Karl along with us. That is . . .' the light died from her face as she grimaced, 'if I can prise him away from Nanny Bar. She might insist on coming along. Maybe you'll see for yourself just how little they trust me with my own son. Shall I organise it for tomorrow?'

Juli glanced at Howard, who said, 'Yes, go ahead. Lyana has to leave in the morning, anyway—she's got another assignment—so we might as well call it a day. I'm happy with what we've done.'

'Fine,' Sara said, and went to rescue Karl from getting entangled in electric cables.

'She's a sweet kid,' Howard said, easing the knees of his jeans before crouching beside Juli. 'But she's out of her depth here. How did she come to be mixed up with the von Remmens?'

'She fell in love with Heini. Now she's stuck with his family.'

'And doesn't she get on with them? I've noticed some needle between her and Madame.'

Juli sat back on her heels, wearily sweeping her hair from her eyes. 'It's Karl who's the bone of contention. Last time I was here, Sara was almost paranoid about it. But she seems to have improved. That's the first time I've heard her mention—Ouch!' She had been fastening a stiff buckle. Her hand slipped and a sharp edge sliced across her thumb. The resulting cut wasn't deep, but it bled freely, causing a

109

concerned Howard to produce a clean handkerchief with which he bound the wound.

'You ought to wash it,' he said, helping her to her feet. 'Have you got any plasters in your room?'

His solicitude touched Juli, and for no reason at all she found her voice hoarse. 'Yes. Don't fuss.'

'I'm not fussing, I'm only trying to take care of you.' A hand under her chin made her look at him and when he saw her distress his expression turned anxious. 'Does it hurt that much?'

'It hardly hurts at all!' she exclaimed, pulling away from him in irritation.

But Howard caught her shoulder. 'Juli, this can't go on. Can't you tell me what's wrong? Ever since we've been here, you've been so uptight I can't get near you. I thought we were friends.'

'We are,' she croaked. 'Howard . . . I'm being a drag. I'm sorry.'

His arm slipped round her. 'There's nothing to apologise for. If it was in my power to make you happy . . . Is there anything I can do? Anything at all?'

Unable to stop herself, she leaned on him, needing human contact more than anything. His arms were the wrong arms, but he was warm and strong and she was grateful for his affection even while she felt guilty about accepting it when she couldn't return it. He held her tenderly, his head bent to hers, his hand smoothing her hair.

'I'd gladly spend the rest of my life taking care of you,' he vowed solemnly, 'if only you'd let me.'

Juli's skin prickled uncomfortably with pity and regret. How she wished he hadn't said that. She eased away from him, looking up into sad blue eyes that knew what her answer would be. 'Howard . . .'

A high-pitched cry from Karl shrilled across the ballroom. 'Uncle Andreas!' he shrieked in delight as he broke from his game and ran full-tilt across the room.

When Juli glanced beyond Howard's shoulder she felt as though her heart had turned a somersault and jumped into her throat, where it throbbed uncomfortably. A few feet inside the doorway, Andreas stood with his head tilted in that habitual listening pose.

Andreas! What was he doing here?

A hot flush coursed through Juli's veins and along all her nerves, followed by a chill as her emotions gyrated wildly. Joy, dismay, hope, anger . . . Everything faded into insignificance beside the sight of the one man whose very presence made her world come alive. He was casually dressed in a sweater and slacks, wearing his dark glasses.

'Hello, Karl!' he laughed as the child wrapped himself round his legs, then he bent and swung Karl up.

Just for a moment, Juli envied the child his place in Andreas's affections, and in his arms.

'Andreas!' Lyana came gliding in soft-soled shoes, her lovely face alight with pleasure. She murmured again, 'Andreas!' and laid her hands on his arm as she reached on tip-toe to kiss his cheek. 'I'm so glad you've come. I was afraid I might miss you. I have to leave early in the morning. Oh, it's lovely to see you!'

'You, too, Lyana,' he replied with a smile. 'Who else is here?'

'Oh . . .' she glanced round the room. 'Everyone. Sara, Nanny Bar, Howard and Julienne. You won't have met Howard yet. Howard . . .' She beckoned to him to come. 'This is Andreas von Remmen. Andreas, this is Howard Marston.'

Shifting Karl to his left arm, Andreas formally shook hands with Howard, full of charm and bonhomie, apparently at ease as he asked how the work was progressing.

Then Sara joined him, taking her son away from him; she, Karl and the nanny departed, but Lyana remained, her hands round Andreas's arm, her flower-pretty face registering her pleasure at his arrival. But the affection between them was platonic; even Juli had learned that. She need never have worried about Andreas's relationship with Lyana.

He was saying, 'I hope I didn't interrupt anything?'

'No, we'd finished for the day,' Howard said. 'We were just packing away.' He glanced at Juli as if wondering why she hung back and said nothing, and she realised that if she didn't make a move it would become obvious that Andreas was the cause of her odd behaviour.

Hoisting the heavy metal case on its shoulder strap, she said brightly, 'There! That's got everything, I think. Herr von Remmen . . . how are you?'

'Thank you, Mrs Blake, I'm well,' he replied with grave courtesy. 'And you?' He held out a hand, giving her no choice but to go closer and greet him, though the instant their fingers touched she knew she had made a mistake. The old magic was still working for her, making a jolt like electricity run up her arm to unsettle her heart. And instead of letting her go Andreas tightened his hold, exploring the binding round her thumb.

'You're hurt?' he asked.

Aware that Howard and Lyana were interested spectators, Juli twisted free of that disturbing grip. 'It's nothing. Just a slight cut. Howard lent me his handkerchief.'

'Have you cleaned it properly?' he asked. 'You must be careful with cuts. Please . . . go and do it at once. And you, Mr Marston— you'll join us for aperitifs.' Typically, he was issuing instructions rather than making requests.

'Thank you,' Howard said, adding

113

meaningfully, 'I could do with a drink.' The look he shot at Juli told her that his need of alcohol was her fault. What the hell is the matter with you? the look said.

'Julienne . . .' Andreas's voice drew her attention back to him. 'We shall be in my sitting-room in the west turret. Join us when you've attended to your hand.'

'Oh, I . . . I want to have a bath,' she muttered. 'I'll give drinks a miss, if you don't mind. I'll see you all at dinner.'

*   *   *

Dinner that night was an apparently relaxed occasion which, for Juli, seethed with hidden tensions. Howard kept watching her, though she avoided meeting his eyes, and Andreas persisted in including her in conversations when he must have known perfectly well that she didn't feel like talking. He seemed determined to torment her, to remind her of his presence. Juli was sure that everyone around that table must be aware of the constraint between her and the master of Falkenruhe.

As soon as the meal was over she made excuses and went to her room without waiting for coffee. She put on her nightgown and a negligée, intending to sit in bed and read, but she couldn't settle. Eventually she put out the light and went to sit by the window and watch the last of the afterglow fade behind the mountain, leaving the Falkenburg ruins etched sharply against the deepening blue of the sky.

Why had Andreas changed his plans and come home so soon? Just to prove that he was no longer interested in her? Or perhaps she was foolish to imagine that his motives had anything to do with her—in Andreas von Remmen's life she was of very little significance.

When someone tapped on her door she didn't answer at once. She didn't feel in the mood to talk to anyone. But after a moment the knock came again and Franz's voice said softly, 'Mrs Blake?'

Sighing, Juli left the window-seat and switched on a lamp by the bed before going to open the door. Franz's face was as inscrutable as ever, the ice-blue eyes steady on hers.

'Mrs Blake . . . Herr von Remmen asks that you join him in his apartments, if it is convenient. He wishes to talk to you.'

'It's not convenient,' Juli replied.

'Is that what you wish me to tell him?' he asked.

'You can tell him whatever you please. I've absolutely nothing to say to Herr von Remmen. Except . . .' As a thought occurred to her she half closed the door and went to the bedside locker, where she had been keeping the jewellery box containing the topaz necklace. She took it back to Franz, thrusting

115

it at him, but Franz only looked at it, and at her. 'Take it!' she insisted. 'Tell Herr von Remmen I can't possibly accept such a gift. I was going to leave it behind when we left, but now that he's here . . .'

Franz kept his hands by his sides, his face wiped clean of expression. 'He went to much trouble to find that for you, Mrs Blake.'

'*He* did, or *you* did?'

A brief flicker of reproach crossed his face. 'The idea of buying a necklace to match your ring was Herr von Remmen's. If he had been able to choose it by himself, he would have done so.'

Juli bit back a desire to trade arguments with the man. She wished she had hidden her resentment of him better. 'I still can't take it. Here—give it back to him.'

'I'm afraid I must refuse,' said Franz, backing away. 'If you wish to return the gift, you will have to do it yourself. I'm sorry to have disturbed you, Mrs Blake. *Gute Nacht.*'

Left standing in the doorway, still holding the jewellery box, Juli retreated and closed the door sharply. How dare the man make her feel guilty? Andreas's infirmity had nothing to do with any of this.

*　　　*　　　*

Only a few minutes later, another soft knock sounded on the door, making Juli stare across

116

the room with her heart thudding in her throat. The knock came again, louder, sounding peremptory. This time, she guessed, Andreas hadn't sent his emissary; he had come in person.

'Go away,' she said in a low voice, drawn across the room to lean on the door, torn between anger and despair. Part of her wanted to open the door, to throw herself into his arms. But she had some pride. She closed her eyes, almost embracing the door. 'Go away!'

'Juli?' came a voice she knew well. Howard's voice. 'Juli, are you all right?'

Swallowing a sob of rueful laughter at the irony of the situation, she opened the door. 'Oh, it's you, Howard. Come in.'

'Who were you expecting?' he asked.

'No one.' She returned to the window-seat, from where she could still see the black outline of the Falkenburg rearing against a sky where a few stars were twinkling in the soft spring night.

There was a long silence and she heard the door close softly. Dimly in the window she could see Howard's reflection in the light from a pink lamp, his fair head lowered, his hands stuck in the pockets of his dark suit. 'It's probably none of my business, but—'

'You're right, Howard,' Juli broke in. 'So please don't ask.'

'It's von Remmen, isn't it?' he persisted. 'How long have you known him, Juli?'

The question surprised her and she turned her head to look at him, unaware of how pale and strained she looked. 'You know how long—since February.'

'That's a lie! You took that picture long before February.'

Juli could only stare at him, her mind blank. 'Picture?'

'The photograph you've got hidden away in your darkroom like some guilty secret!'

A chill ran through Juli. That photograph . . . she had forgotten Howard had seen it.

Slowly, he came away from the door and walked towards her, pausing by the ottoman at the end of the bed. His face was flushed, his movements so controlled that she knew he had had too much to drink. 'I'm right, aren't I?' he demanded. 'As soon as he walked in I knew I'd seen him somewhere, but the answer didn't strike me until after dinner, when he took those dark glasses off and . . . If you hadn't met him before February, how come you've got a picture of him, heh?'

She looked down at her hands, spreading them out and seeing how they were trembling. 'That's a long story, Howard.'

'I'll *bet* it is!' Two strides brought him close enough to grab her by the shoulders and jerk her to her feet. 'You should have told me! I'd never have asked you to come here if I'd known. What was he to you—boyfriend? Lover?'

'It's not like that!' she croaked. 'I didn't even know his full name. He blazed across my sky like lightning and then he was gone. I don't know why I kept the photo. I thought I'd never see him again. When he turned up at the airport here to meet me, I could hardly believe my eyes.'

'And is that all you've got to say?'

'What else do you want?' Pulling free of him, she went over to the dressing-table, her fingers stroking the top of the jewellery case containing the topaz necklace.

'I want to know what's been happening between you,' Howard said. 'The way you've been behaving . . . you're in love with him, aren't you?'

She might have given a dozen different answers, but suddenly she found it impossible to be anything but honest. 'I'm not sure.'

There was a long, long silence before he replied, 'You mean you haven't admitted it to yourself yet.'

'I mean I'm not sure!' She glanced at him over her shoulder, troubled by his mood. This narrow-eyed, angry Howard was a stranger to her. 'I thought we might have a chance of making something out of our relationship, but . . .' She opened the jewellery case and took the necklace out, tawny topazes warm against the cool shine of silver. 'He had other ideas. He sent me this as a goodbye gift.'

'Then why did he turn up today?' Howard

demanded. 'He must have known you were still here.'

'I don't *know* why!' Juli cried. 'I don't know anything any more. I don't understand him at all.'

Howard came to examine the necklace. When he looked at Juli, his face was contorted by disgust and scorn. 'That's quite a sweetener. Just how far has this relationship gone?'

Incensed, she snatched the necklace from him, glaring at him over it with eyes brighter than the stones. 'I think you should go now, Howard. There are limits to what friendship allows.'

'And what did you allow *him*?' he grated. His hands fastened on her upper arms as he jerked her in close to him.

Juli struggled ineffectually, her thoughts sluggish with distress and disbelief. 'Howard . . . Howard, don't do this! It's not you.'

'Maybe it's the real me,' he said hoarsely.

She twisted her head away, horribly aware of being alone with him in a bedroom far from other occupants of the castle. 'Please!' she begged him. 'Please don't, Howard. You don't mean this. Please!!' Her voice rose in a yelp as his mouth plunged for hers.

Several things happened at once: the door crashed back; a harsh voice said '*Schon gut!* That's enough!' and Juli found herself released from that terrible embrace, the back of her hand cooling her crushed lips. Howard spun round, swaying a little as he stared at the intruder.

Blinking away the mist in her eyes, Juli saw Andreas standing there, his expression colder than she had ever seen it. He was still wearing the black trousers he had worn at dinner, but he had removed his jacket and tie—and his dark glasses. His white evening shirt was half open, revealing a glimpse of tanned skin beneath.

'Marston,' he said in a low voice that shook with contained fury. 'I think the lady would like you to leave.'

Pulling his jacket straight, Howard started for the door. 'I was just going.' He paused in front of Andreas, saying bitterly, 'She may think she's in love with you, but what she's really feeling is pity. And when she gets over it I'll be there waiting. So don't think you've won, von Remmen. Your triumph is only temporary.'

He pushed past Andreas, striding from the room. In his wake, the room sang with silence. Juli felt sick, wondering how Howard could be so vicious—Howard, of all people. She had seen a side of him that night that she would never have believed was part of his nature.

Into the silence Andreas said, 'Did he hurt you?'

She shook her head, then realising that wasn't enough she cleared her throat and managed, 'No. No, I'm all right, thank you. He

121

wasn't really . . . I mean, I think he'd had too much to drink.'

'Sometimes it's the only comfort a man can find. I hope you'll forgive him, Julienne.'

Hardly believing her ears, Juli searched his face but found no clue as to why he should plead Howard's cause; Andreas had become skilled at hiding all his feelings. 'I probably will,' she said. 'I'll forgive him, but I shall never feel the same about him.'

'Perhaps that's good. Perhaps you needed to be broken of old habits. Lyana has told me that Marston is very fond of you.'

'We're just friends!' Juli exclaimed. 'We shall never be anything more, as far as I'm concerned. Don't think you can salve your conscience by foisting me off on to Howard.'

His brow furrowed. 'Excuse me? My conscience? What do you mean?'

'You know very well what I mean!' She was too hurt and angry to conceal her feelings any longer. 'Isn't that what the necklace was about—your way of paying me off, as if I were just another mercenary woman out for anything she can get? Which reminds me . . .' She grabbed up the necklace, laying it back in its box. 'You'd better take this, since you're here. I can't accept it.'

But when she went closer to him he stood immobile, as though he didn't understand. She had to reach for his hand and put the box in it, the contact unbearably painful to her. Only

122

then, as she stepped away, did she look up and see how bleak his face had gone, his eyes closed and bitter lines about his mouth. The sight made her heart want to weep.

'You don't like it?' he said.

'Of course I like it!' she croaked. 'It's beautiful. I just can't accept such a gift from you.'

'Why?'

'Why?' she echoed, torn between bursting into tears and throwing herself at him in a passion of anger and hurt. 'If you don't know why then you must be totally insensitive. And don't look like that! *I'm* the one who's hurting! It was just a game to you, right from the start. Right from that first night at Sharborough House.'

'No!' he denied. 'No, Julienne, that is not so!'

She found herself close to him, her hand on his arm, watching his face work as he struggled with some fierce emotion that was painful to see. 'I wish I could believe that,' she breathed. 'I wish I knew what you were really thinking. I wish I knew what you really wanted. Do you know it yourself?'

'It is not what I want that is of importance,' he said hoarsely. 'It is the way I know it must be.'

'I don't understand.'

'I know,' was all he said.

'Then explain to me!' Juli cried. 'Why didn't

you come to see me when you were in London? Why did you run off to New York?'

A sound escaped him that was half-laugh, half-sigh. 'At the time, I thought it was for the best. But, as you see, I couldn't stay away. I despise the weakness I find in myself. I have only made difficulties for you by coming home.'

'Difficulties?'

'For you, and Marston,' he said. 'I heard what he was saying to you in the ballroom. He was offering you marriage.'

'You also heard what was going on only a few minutes ago!' Juli reminded him. 'Do you need any more proof that, however he feels, I certainly don't feel the same?'

'Perhaps not, not yet. But given time—'

'No!' The cry was torn out of her. 'Don't say it! Why do you want me to turn to Howard? Why are you afraid to get involved? Oh, Andreas, what dreadful thing did Marie-Elizabeth do to hurt you so?'

He stiffened, his face seeming to close up against her as his arm brushed her aside, forcing her away from him. 'Marie-Elizabeth was Marie-Elizabeth,' he said flatly. 'She was no longer capable of hurting me, however much she tried. It's not because of her that . . .' He stopped himself, his lips compressed as if he would never finish the thought out loud.

'Then why?' Juli asked in an urgent undertone. '*Why*, Andreas?'

'Because . . .' The words seemed to be forced out of him, harsh with fury. 'Because I have made up my mind! That's why! You don't know me, Julienne. I'm not a fairy-tale prince. Not Lohengrin. I'm arrogant, I'm demanding, I have an evil temper which has got worse since this!' A sweep of his hand indicated the darkness behind his eyes. 'Marston was right—you're sorry for me. Do you know how that makes me feel—to be an object of pity? Go away from here. Go before we hurt each other any more. Please . . . make your peace with Howard Marston. You'll be happier that way. And keep this.' He tossed the necklace in its case to the floor as he opened the door. 'It's of no use to me.'

CHAPTER SEVEN

It seemed to Juli that she hardly slept. The scenes of the previous day kept revolving in her mind, playing over and over, always leading to the same ending: Andreas had rejected her, told her to go away.

After an endless night, the sky began to lighten. The sun rose. Another day had to be faced. She showered and dressed automatically, wishing she could escape without seeing anyone, wishing she could just go home and forget everything that had happened.

Making her way along the corridors, she paused as she saw Howard sitting at the top of a flight of stairs, waiting for her. He eased himself to his feet, having trouble meeting her eyes. Faint colour stained his cheeks as he said, 'How do I apologise?'

'You can't,' Juli said, unable to bring herself to relieve him of his guilt. 'Let's not mention it again.'

For a moment he studied her face unhappily. 'You're never going to forgive me, are you? I was drunk, Juli. I didn't mean anything by it. I was crazy jealous, that's all.'

'Yes, I know,' she sighed. 'And I'm sorry for it. But I can't feel the way you want me to feel, Howard. You must know that.'

'I suppose I do.' He stuffed his hands in his pockets and let his shoulders slump. 'I've only got myself to blame. It's just that I've always hoped that my chance might come one day. And then to find that you've fallen for someone else . . .' He glanced up at her through his lashes, as if he had hoped to hear her deny any feeling for Andreas. When she said nothing, he sighed to himself. 'So what'll you do? Stay here with him?'

The tears she had fought all night came tugging behind her eyes, though with an effort she kept her voice steady, 'Hardly. To do that I'd need some sign that I'd be welcome. As it is . . . I've been firmly ordered to leave.'

'He's sending you away?' Howard said incredulously. 'Why?'

'Because he doesn't want me. After all, I'm not in his league, am I?' Hearing the bitter cynicism that had crept into her voice, she stopped herself, knowing that she didn't mean it. She had sensed the pain in Andreas—a pain as deep as her own. He was sending her away because he *did* care, not because he didn't. But she still didn't understand why it had to be that way.

A voice from below cried, Juli is that you?' and Sara hurried into sight, lifting a reddened face and tear-strewn eyes as she began to climb the stairs. 'I *told you* we wouldn't be allowed to get away from this lousy place even for an hour or two!' she choked. 'Nanny Bar won't let Karl come with us. She says he's got a cold. A cold! As if it would hurt him to have some fresh air on a lovely day like this! And Madame's backing her up. They don't trust me with him. Nobody thinks I'm fit to be his mother! Oh, Juli . . .'

Juli caught hold of the girl, letting Sara lean against her as sobs tore through her. Across her bent head, Juli sent a troubled look at the bewildered Howard. 'It's all right, I'll deal with this.'

'Did you mean what you said about leaving as soon as possible?' he asked. 'Shall I phone and see if we can get a flight some time today?'

'Yes, do that,' Juli said.

As Howard hurried away, Sara slowly lifted her head to stare at Juli with drowned eyes. 'You're leaving?'

'You knew we were leaving in a day or so, anyway.'

'Then we're never going to have that outing!'

Momentarily Juli felt she couldn't cope with more complications. She had enough to think about already. She wanted to get away. Sara von Remmen was not her concern. But she couldn't just brush the girl aside. 'We'll have to settle for a compromise,' she said. 'If we can't get out for a drive, why don't we go . . . say for a walk—up to the Falkenburg? We can talk in private there.'

'That's not the point!' Sara cried, breaking

128

away from Juli's grasp. 'I want to get away from here, just for an hour, but they won't let me—don't you see that? I'm a prisoner! Oh . . . you still don't believe me, do you? You think I'm hysterical. But it's true, Juli! Prove it for yourself. You go and ask if we can take Karl for a drive. Go and ask Madame. Go now, while she's still at breakfast.'

Unable to think of a good reason to refuse this challenge, Juli sighed, 'Very well—if only to prove to you that you're over-reacting to this whole thing. Nobody's keeping you prisoner, Sara.'

They found Madame Ghislaine alone at breakfast with a morning newspaper which she folded and set aside to smile at Juli. For a fleeting instant her expression darkened as she saw Sara in the doorway but then her face cleared again and she lifted the silver coffee pot.

'Join me, my dear. I had hoped to breakfast with Lyana, but she had a very early start. Coffee?'

'Thank you, but . . .' Juli remained on her feet, wishing that Sara wouldn't skulk behind her. 'Forgive me, Madame, but may I ask you . . . is it true that you object to our taking Karl out?'

Madame's eyes had gone opaque as her glance flitted away and she delicately pressed a white linen napkin to a corner of her mouth. 'Karl has a chill. If Miss Entwhistle says he's

129

not fit enough to be taken out, then I shall not argue.'

'He's only got a bit of a sniffle!' Sara said.

'But we employ the nanny to decide on such matters,' Madame replied. 'I shall not argue with you, Sara. You're a silly, selfish girl. You don't really want Karl with you—you merely want to defy me. Isn't that so?'

Sara stepped forward, hands clenched into fists as she said through her teeth. 'He's my son! Mine, not yours!'

Every ounce of warmth left Madame's face. Very slowly, with an awful controlled anger, she rose to her full imperious height, her eyes like stones in her pale face. But before she could speak another voice joined in—Andreas's voice, saying from the doorway, 'Must we start a new day with disagreements in front of a guest?'

Suddenly drum-taut with nerves, Juli glanced round as he came in, casually dressed and wearing his dark glasses, with Franz not far behind.

'Then you deal with it!' Madame Ghislaine rasped. 'I am tired of these constant battles.'

As she swept from the room, Andreas made his way to his usual chair. Sara's mutinous gaze followed him. 'Well, go ahead,' she challenged. 'Now you tell me Karl's not fit enough to go for a drive.'

'Is he unwell?' Andreas asked.

'Apart from the snuffles, no.'

'Then I see no reason why he cannot be taken for a drive,' Andreas said. 'Wrap him up warmly, in case of cold winds, and—'

'You mean we can go?' Sara asked incredulously.

'Of course. Why not? I'm sure Mrs Blake would enjoy a sightseeing trip. You may all go. Take the limousine. Franz will drive you.'

Juli had been assuring herself the whole thing was a storm in a teacup, but Franz's name struck a chill. The manservant with his cold eyes and watchful manner was not a comfortable companion.

Evidently Sara felt something of the same reaction; her face went deathly pale and then flushed to fire. 'We don't want to go with Franz. We want to go by ourselves—just Juli and me, and Karl. Just for one short afternoon so I can get away from this place, and you, and everything here. Don't you have any human feelings, Andreas? I'm going crazy shut up here!'

'But you are not shut up,' Andreas said, a sudden edge in his voice, as if he were tired of her arguments. 'I have just offered you the chance of an outing. Go where you like. Enjoy yourselves.'

'With Franz along?' Sara demanded.

'Of course with Franz along! That's the function of a chauffeur.'

'It's also the function of a watchdog—a jailer.' But the fight was seeping out of Sara.

She turned to Juli, her mouth wry with bitterness and her eyes awash with fresh tears. 'Maybe you believe me now. If I want to take my son for an outing I always have to have an escort. He's too precious to be left in the care of his own mother!'

Juli found Franz watching her with pale hooded eyes. Andreas sat still, his face impassive, as if made of rock, like his mountain.

'I can't believe you mean this,' Juli told him. 'What harm could possibly come to Karl if Sara and I were both there? I can understand your being protective, but—'

'I am the master of this house,' Andreas broke in, his voice cool and dismissive, 'and I make the decisions that affect my family. I should be grateful, Mrs Blake, if you would remember that you are a guest here at Falkenruhe.'

Feeling as though she had been slapped, she straightened, her face growing hot with humiliation. She could hardly believe that Andreas could use that tone of voice on her. Why, he himself had involved her in Sara's troubles, had asked her advice, confided his fears. Now suddenly the door was slammed in her face.

But before she could find words to answer him he went on, 'However, perhaps I am being a little too cautious. As you say, with two of you to watch over him, Karl should be safe enough. So . . . very well. Go for an outing. I should hate you to take away the impression that I am not a reasonable man.'

Sara clutched at Juli's arm, her wide eyes fixed on Andreas's impassive face. 'You mean, we can go? Just the two of us, with Karl?'

'I trust you will not make me regret it,' Andreas said.

'Oh, I won't!' Sara's tears had dried and now her face was bright. 'Oh, that's great! Thank you, Andreas. I'll go and tell Karl right away.'

In the silence following Sara's departure, Juli hovered uncertainly, not sure what to do. 'That was kind of you,' she said. 'And I promise you we *will* take good care of Karl.'

'I'm sure you will,' he replied, and gestured across the table. 'Please . . . sit down and eat something. While you are here, allow me the pleasure of your company.'

Juli sank into a chair and Franz moved to pour her a cup of coffee. She found his presence inhibiting, but with so little time left she had to speak up. 'I was under the impression that my company was no longer wanted,' she said.

'You know that is not so, Julienne,' the answer came soft and sad.

She found the hairs on her nape standing up in response to the sound of her name on his lips, spoken in the soft, intimate way that had always disturbed her: *'Zhu-lee-enne.'*

'I know nothing of the kind!' she responded.

A glance at Franz discovered him standing detached, as if he were both deaf and blind. Since he was neither, it was impossible to hold a personal conversation with him in the room. Perhaps that was why Andreas let the man stay—to prevent any argument. Evidently he had not changed his mind.

A footfall sounded on the parquet along the corridor and Howard appeared, momentarily disconcerted by finding her with Andreas, then he said, 'I've been on to the airport. They have two seats available on the evening flight. We have to be there by seven.'

'That's fine,' Juli said. 'That will give me time to go for a drive with Sara and Karl. We'll leave for the airport as soon as I get back.'

'You're leaving today?' Andreas asked, his voice suddenly strained though his face was devoid of expression.

'Our work is done,' Juli replied, forcing herself to be brisk and matter of fact. 'We mustn't outstay our welcome. You *did* say you wanted me to leave, didn't you?'

She waited for his reply but when it came it brought no comfort.

'It will be best for everyone.'

'Then if you'll excuse me I'll go and do my packing,' Juli said, throwing her napkin aside, unable to bear being in the same room with him any longer. 'I don't think I want any breakfast.'

That afternoon, driving a silver Scirocco borrowed from the selection of vehicles at Falkenruhe, Juli played chauffeur to Sara and Karl—who, if he had a cold, seemed remarkably unaffected by it. The little boy was safely strapped in the back seat, and Juli had every intention of being ultra careful in her driving: while Karl and Sara were in her charge she would make sure they remained safe.

'You can take us to see one of the loveliest valleys in this area,' Sara chatted, more animated than Juli had ever seen her. 'Turn left here, then first right. It used to be our favourite place—Heini's and mine. Oh, isn't it wonderful to get away? I could hardly believe my ears when Andreas finally agreed, though he wouldn't have done it if *you* hadn't been involved. And I don't think Madame was very pleased about it. Did you feel the atmosphere at lunch?—You could have cut it with a knife.'

Juli had indeed been aware of undercurrents, a swirl of mixed emotions covered by conventional politenesses. But one good thing had emerged over the mid-day meal—Madame Ghislaine's announcement that the 'Chéri' boutiques would be buying HM's winter collection. So some good had come from this whole sorry affair.

Their route lay through pretty lanes and forested hills. The roadsides were decked in wildflowers and a haze of green lay over every tree and bush, making Juli regret that she would not see Luxembourg later in the season. There was a great deal she would have liked to see and learn about this lovely country, if only circumstances had been different.

She was so abstracted by her thoughts that it was a while before she noticed that the same car had been following her for several miles— almost from the gates of Falkenruhe, now that she thought about it. It was visible only in occasional glimpses along the twisting lanes, a low-slung sports car with dark paintwork that might have been forest green. Since Juli was driving only at moderate speed, she expected the faster vehicle to overtake, but it hung behind, never fully visible in the rear-view mirror.

Reluctant to worry Sara, Juli said nothing about that following car. Andreas's paranoia over Karl must have got to her. She couldn't believe the vehicle posed a real threat. But just to be sure she slowed down even more, keeping an eye on the road behind. The green car appeared again, but almost at once turned off down a side road. Breathing a silent sigh of relief, Juli increased her speed and berated herself for having an overheated imagination

'We're almost there,' Sara said. 'Look, there's the sign. Follow the track down to the car park.'

The track led down among trees to an open area well hidden from the road. Here a couple of cars were parked; it was too early in the year for crowds of tourists.

The beauty spot consisted of a deep, wooded gorge silvered by many small waterfalls tumbling from rocky cliffs to plunge into dark pools overhung by trees. Stepped pathways twined steeply up and down beneath overhanging branches and shoulders of granite, and here were hidden snowdrops, primroses and violets.

With Karl safely holding a hand of each, Juli and Sara explored the sun-dappled pathways and shadowy nooks.

'I think I ought to get Karl to a toilet before we go any further,' Sara said as they reached a place where the path forked, one branch leading down into the depths of the narrow gorge while the other ran back up towards the car park. 'Why don't you go on and we'll catch you up?'

Before Juli could reply, Sara was heading off with Karl, climbing up a stepped path that angled across the hillside. Juli remained where she was, torn between going on or following Sara. She felt vaguely uneasy about letting the pair out of her sight.

But hardly had Sara vanished than she reappeared, hurrying now, with many glances behind her. Karl was going too slowly for her;

she swept him up into her arms and came on down the pathway.

'What's wrong?' Juli asked.

'Sssh!' came the frantic rejoinder. 'Franz is up there! I saw him!'

'Franz?' Juli echoed in disbelief. 'Are you trying to tell me he followed us?'

'He must have done!' Sara's eyes were wide with fright as she set Karl on his feet and laid hold of his hand. 'I told you he's forever spying on me.'

Juli remembered the green sports car which had appeared to be tailing her. 'Oh, surely Andreas wouldn't send him to—'

'What makes you think Andreas knows about it?' Sara cried. 'Juli . . . I don't like this. What is he doing skulking up there? I've never trusted him. Heini didn't like him, either. Suppose he's been waiting, biding his time. He knew we'd be out alone this afternoon. What if he tries to snatch Karl?'

'Why should he do that?'

'For the ransom money, of course! The von Remmens are worth a fortune. Juli, I'm scared. I'm going to try and get back to the car and lock myself in. Will you try to distract Franz?—let him see you, and draw him away from us. It should be easy enough among all these paths. Oh, please! Help me save my baby!'

A man's figure appeared higher up the hill, beyond branches wearing sprays of young leaves. Sara caught her breath in alarm and Juli responded instinctively, knowing she must guard Karl. There was no time to think about it logically.

'This way!'

It became like a deadly game of hide-and-seek among steep pathways and tall, sheltering trees and rockfaces. Franz *was* there. He *was* following them. Juli caught glimpses of him among the trees.

Somewhere down in the gorge, Sara and Karl took a branch-shaded pathway like a tunnel, which hid their flight back up the hill. Juli continued on down, showing herself just often enough for Franz to follow. Among the burgeoning growth she hoped it would be some time before her pursuer realised she was alone.

After a while she paused, her heart thudding uncomfortably as she backed under an overhang of rock, aware that Franz was out of sight above her. By now Sara and Karl must have made it to the car. Juli waited a moment to catch her breath, then ran head down beneath the cover of shrubs to another fork in the path which headed once more upwards. With any luck, it would take Franz a few minutes to discover she had changed direction. She could be back at the car and safely on the road to Falkenruhe before he realised he had been outwitted.

She was gasping for breath, her legs aching.

Slowly the sky opened above her. Near the top of the gorge she came to a pathway from which the ground fell away steeply to the right. She stopped, a pulse throbbing in her throat.

A man stood on the path several yards ahead of her, barring her way—a tall man, wearing dark glasses and carrying a long walking-stick. Andreas! Juli's head reeled with exhaustion and bewilderment. What was Andreas doing here?

He must have heard her. She saw him stop and cock his head to listen. Out of breath, and totally confused by what was happening, Juli croaked, 'Andreas! What—'

A shout from below drew her attention. It was Franz, hidden among the growth on the hill, calling something in German that to Juli was unintelligible, but it made Andreas catch his breath and swear succinctly. He took a long stride towards Juli, going dangerously near the edge of the path. 'Where are they? Where are they, Julienne? *Du liebe Gott*—'

At the same moment, from behind him, Karl's high voice called, 'Uncle Andreas! Uncle Andreas!'

Juli glimpsed the boy, and Sara, who was dragging her son away. But it was no more than a glimpse. The child's cry had distracted Andreas, disoriented him. He turned sharply, off balance. He caught his foot on a stone. His shoe slipped on a crumbling edge.

'Andreas!!' Even as Juli started forward to

140

save him, he fell. Her own scream rang in her ears. She would never forget the echoes tossed mockingly along the gorge, nor the sound of breaking branches, nor the sight of his body tumbling, sliding . . . She stood above and watched, helpless, wincing at every jolt. She felt the final sickening jerk as a tree trunk broke his fall. Andreas lay sprawled there, unmoving.

She never remembered scrambling down that steep hillside. Only later did she discover the cuts and grazes on her hands, arms and legs, and the inexplicable black bruise on her hip. She knelt beside Andreas, seeing his face white as death, seeing blood trickling from a wound on his head. He was unconscious. Was he breathing?

As she reached out towards him, a rough hand grabbed her shoulder and spun her away. 'Don't move him!' Franz's ice-blue eyes glared hatred at her as he bent beside his employer, feeling for a pulse.

After a moment he got to his feet saying, 'Stay here. I must telephone for an ambulance.'

Kneeling there on the stony hillside, Juli held Andreas's cold hand between her own as through a glaze of tears she watched his still face. You can't die, she kept thinking. You can't leave me. I won't let you go. Please, Andreas, don't die. Andreas . . .

She didn't comprehend what was

happening. Sara would come back at any minute, surely? She must have seen what had happened. But Sara didn't come. It was all a part of the Alice-in-Wonderland unreality of that afternoon's events.

Eventually, Franz returned, saying, 'They're coming. How is he?'

Juli shook her head. Her voice was a thread. 'I don't know, Franz. I don't know.' And then, 'Where's Sara? Why hasn't she come?'

The silence stretched, understitched by the song of merry birds. Juli looked at the manservant and found his face unreadable. 'I said—where's Sara?' she repeated.

'Frau Sara is gone,' he said flatly. 'Do you pretend not to know anything, Mrs Blake? You who persuaded Herr von Remmen to trust you with Karl? You—who played decoy to distract me while Frau Sara got away with the boy?'

'What?' She gaped at him, bewildered.

'But she will not go far,' he said. 'The police will find her. I telephoned them, as well as the ambulance.'

Before she had a chance to think about this information she heard a siren wailing, coming closer. Help was at hand. Thank God.

When the medical team arrived Juli became an onlooker in a drama whose outcome meant so much to her she hardly dared think of it. She kept her eyes on Andreas's face, praying for a sign of life, but he remained still, white-faced, as he was strapped on to a stretcher and borne away.

After the ambulance had gone, Juli was stupidly surprised to find the silver Scirocco missing from the car park.

'Frau Sara took it,' Franz said.

'Sara?' she echoed blankly. 'But she told me she couldn't drive!'

His face expressed his impatience with her naivety. 'And did you believe her, Mrs Blake?' Without waiting for an answer, he gestured across the park. 'We will use the Ferrari.'

The Ferrari was forest green—the same car that Juli had seen on the road. Andreas and Franz had been in it; they *had* been following her and Sara. But to guard the child, not to harm him. Belatedly, Juli was beginning to realise that she had been duped, tricked into helping Sara 'escape', with her son, from the von Remmens.

'Andreas knew this might happen, didn't he?' she said, feeling sick. 'Why didn't he warn me?'

'It is not my place to make explanations,' Franz said.

'Well, will you at least tell me where you're taking me? Are we going to the hospital?'

'To Falkenruhe. Madame Ghislaine must be informed. And you, Mrs Blake, have a plane to catch.'

The reminder silenced Juli. Franz seemed to hold her responsible for what had happened. Would Andreas blame her, too?

They found Madame closeted in her book-lined study with Howard, who leapt up in concern as he saw Juli, coming to take her hand.

'Jules! You look terrible! Whatever's wrong?'

The conversation which followed, mainly between Franz and Madame Ghislaine, was conducted in rapid Letzburgish and left Madame looking every year of her age. Juli caught only the main drift—that Andreas had been hurt and Sara had vanished. Franz kept mentioning 'Mrs Blake', causing Madame to shoot questioning looks at Juli.

Breaking away from Howard, Juli threw out her hands. 'Madame . . . I don't know exactly what Franz is saying, but I swear to you I didn't realise what was happening. If anything happens to Andreas because of my stupidity . . .' Suddenly her eyes were flooded, her throat so thick with grief that she couldn't go on.

'Child,' Madame's quiet voice came from close at hand and cool fingers touched Juli's cheek. 'Do not distress yourself. I shall go now to the hospital. Will you come with me?'

Juli gaped at her, but before she could find words to express her gratitude Howard put in, 'I'm sorry, Madame, but Juli and I are due to catch the evening flight. We ought to be leaving for the airport now.'

'Perhaps we should let Juli decide that,' Madame said, her calm grey eyes full of understanding as she turned to Juli. 'The choice is yours, my dear. Will you come to the hospital with me, or will you go with Howard?'

'I'll come with you,' Juli said.

'But Jules —'

Howard bit off his protest as she looked at him with clear tawny eyes, saying, 'I'm sorry, Howard. But until I know that Andreas . . . I can't leave yet. I just can't.'

After all, it was as simple as that.

CHAPTER EIGHT

At the hospital, Juli and Madame Ghislaine alighted from the chauffeur-driven Mercedes and Juli turned to take leave of Howard, who was going on to the airport for the evening flight.

'Well, you've done it,' she said lightly. 'Congratulations. Your designs will be in all the Chéri boutiques. Remember what you said— "Howard Marston. London, Paris, Rome . . .".'

'My dream come true,' he replied, but the glance he gave her was full of despondency. 'I wonder if it was worth the price.'

'I'm sorry, Howard.'

'Yes, so am I,' he sighed.

Juli turned away, devoid of words to comfort him. Between herself and Howard, nothing could ever be quite the same. She didn't even watch the Mercedes move away; she was following Madame Ghislaine into the hospital, all her thoughts on Andreas.

They were informed that Andreas was still unconscious. Everything possible was being done for him. The medical staff could offer no further information. There was nothing to do but wait.

In the visitors' waiting area, comfortable chairs stood round tables bearing magazines; there were Brueghel prints on the walls; the place was functional, soulless. Juli perched uneasily on the edge of one of the chairs, flipping through a magazine whose pages might as well have been blank for all she saw of them. Her thoughts veered between hope and terror. Andreas had been so pale, so still. Did he, like Franz, think she had aided and abetted Sara in her deception?

Unable to sit still, she got up again and went to stare out of the window at the view over lawned grounds with the city in the distance.

'I still don't entirely understand what happened this afternoon,' she said. 'Was Sara plotting all the time to run away?'

'Who knows?' Madame Ghislaine sighed. 'But perhaps I should tell you, this is not the first time she has behaved irrationally. We have been afraid that she might attempt to run away again.'

'Again?' Juli swung round, staring at the pale face with its skin stretched over beautiful bone-structure. 'Then why didn't someone warn me?'

'I told Andreas you should know the truth,' Madame said, 'but he said No. He said Sara had changed and it would be unfair of us to speak to you of things that were past.' She grimaced impatiently. 'Andreas has always argued Sara's case. At times he is too kind, too reasonable. At times he is a fool! And now, because of it . . .' Her voice broke in distress and, unable to say more, she searched in her handbag for a handkerchief.

Concerned, Juli went to sit beside her. 'It's my fault. I should have realised what was going on. I was so stupid!'

'You were not to know,' Madame said. 'Andreas believed that Sara would keep her promise. But you see she has betrayed his trust, as she has always betrayed us.' Her face twisted with a mixture of distress and anger, her thin fingers pulling at the fabric of her handkerchief as she stared into the middle distance. 'The girl was never our kind. She hated Falkenruhe. She preferred the city. She was always light-minded. She took my son away from me, and then he died.'

'You can't hold Sara to blame for that,' Juli put in, feeling defensive on Sara's behalf. 'She loved Heini. She must have been devastated when she lost him.'

Madame Ghislaine chose not to hear this argument. 'Oh, we should have made her come to Falkenruhe then. But she wept when we suggested it. Andreas said we should not force her to leave her home, not at such a time. I let him persuade me. But it was a mistake. Within weeks she was disgracing us. She was seeing other men.'

Juli must have caught her breath or made some sound of surprise; Madame's grey eyes focused on her with a faint cynical smile.

'It's true. We discovered it when Andreas went to call on her one evening and found

Karl alone in the apartment. His mother had gone out. It was very late before she came home. She was dressed for a party. She had been drinking. The man with her escaped before Andreas could discover who he was.'

'Is that when you took Karl back to Falkenruhe?' Juli asked.

'For his own safety. It was clear that Sara was not fit to have care of him. We employed Miss Entwhistle to look after Karl. Sara was given the choice—to stay in the city or to come to the Schlossel. It suited her to play the fond mother refusing to be parted from her son. But she made it clear she was not happy. She was bitter, ungrateful, and still Andreas made excuses for her—she was grieving, he said, she was overwrought, she did not know what she was doing . . .

'Then one day, there was a terrible argument. Sara took Karl. She tried to leave. Of course we stopped her. She became hysterical. We had to call a doctor. He said she was suffering from stress.' The handkerchief ripped under her angry fingers. 'That was when we began to be more cautious. We could not trust her with Karl. She thinks of him only as a weapon to use against us.'

'I'm sure that's not true, Madame,' Juli said. 'She loves Karl very much. She's just scared that you might try to take him from her. She's desperately unhappy.'

Madame lifted tear-bright eyes, saying

149

furiously, 'You sound like Andreas! Ah!' The startled exclamation escaped her as she caught sight of someone in the doorway and her beringed hands flew to her throat.

Juli leapt to her feet. Sara had appeared, her hair dishevelled, her face streaked and puffy with tears. But underneath her distress lay a new strength and calmness.

'Juli's right,' she said. 'I've been scared all the time since Heini died.'

'Scared of what?' Andreas's mother snapped.

'Of you, mainly.'

This seemed to surprise Madame Ghislaine, then she stiffened her spine and demanded, 'Where is Karl? What have you done with him?'

'He's safe.' Sara came further into the room and sank into a chair. 'I took him back to Falkenruhe.'

'Falkenruhe?' Juli queried in disbelief.

'Yes, Falkenruhe, where he belongs. I came to my senses, finally. How . . . how is Andreas?'

'Do you care?' Madame demanded.

Fresh tears welled in Sara's eyes. 'Of course I care! I never meant to hurt anyone. Especially not Andreas. At least he's tried to be kind to me, even if I never appreciated it until now. I know I've done wrong. I've been half crazy since I lost Heini. I know you never wanted him to marry me. I've kept thinking that you were planning to take Karl away from me, too.

So I decided to take him away from you.'

That was why she had been so anxious to get away on an 'outing' with Juli, she confessed. She had smuggled a couple of bags down to the car; she had planned to lose Juli in the gorge and be miles away before the alarm was raised. But the arrival of Franz and Andreas had complicated matters.

'I panicked,' Sara admitted, shame-faced. 'All I could think was that I had to get away, at any cost. I was almost at the border before I started to think about it—I'd frightened Karl, caused Andreas to hurt himself . . . And for what? I didn't even know where I was going. I realised that running away never solved anything. So I turned around and came back. Juli . . . can you ever forgive me? I know I shouldn't have made use of your friendship. It was a terrible thing to do.'

'Stupid!' Madame muttered. 'Stupid!'

With tears in her eyes, Sara agreed that stupidity had been her main trait recently. 'It's time I grew up. I intend to try, if you'll help me.'

'Well,' Madame said stiffly. 'Well . . .'

The chasm between the two of them was still wide, Juli thought, but perhaps with a little more tolerance on both sides it might be narrowed. Whatever happened, Sara had shown immense courage by coming back to admit that she had been wrong. Perhaps it was a turning-point.

*　　　*　　　*

After what seemed an interminable wait, a doctor came to inform them that Andreas had regained consciousness, though he was confused and in considerable pain; he would not be allowed visitors until the morning. By some miracle he had escaped with nothing worse than a cracked bone in his leg and concussion; the rest of his injuries were minor cuts and scrapes. He would be kept in hospital for a few days, as a routine precaution.

Madame insisted that she must see her son. The doctor was equally insistent that she could not. The doctor won.

In the darkness of the car, on the way back to Falkenruhe, Juli quietly blotted tears of relief from her face. Only now did she fully realise how afraid she had been. There was no longer any doubt of the depth of her feelings for Andreas von Remmen.

What was in doubt, she thought sadly, was how he felt about her. He kept changing his mind, vacillating, torn between his heart and his head. *You'll be happier with Howard Marston,'* he had said. But that was crazy. Without Andreas she would be desolate.

*　　　*　　　*

Going down to breakfast the following

morning, Juli discovered that Madame Ghislaine had awoken with a blinding migraine that would prevent her from going to the hospital. She had sent instructions that Juli should go in her place.

'You're honoured,' Sara said. 'If she'd been well, she'd have insisted on her right to see Andreas first. She must approve of you. I didn't think any woman would ever be good enough for a son of hers.'

'I'm not sure what you mean,' Juli prevaricated.

'Oh, don't! It's painfully obvious how you feel about him. So go—go and see how he is.'

'Will you be all right?'

'Just fine.' Sara's mouth twisted ruefully. 'Don't worry about me, Juli. I've decided to make the best of things. Besides . . . if you're going to be around, Falkenruhe won't be quite so daunting. You are planning to be around, I take it?'

Juli held up crossed fingers for luck. 'Let's say I'm hoping. All I have to do is convince Andreas he can't do without me.'

In this crusading mood, Juli again borrowed the silver Scirocco and drove into Luxembourg City. She found the hospital without much trouble and was soon following the gleaming corridors and riding in an elevator to an upper floor.

A nurse pointed out the room she wanted.

Outside the door she paused and took a

153

deep breath, smoothing down her light skirt, running a hand over her cap of golden hair. Then she knocked on the door rather harder than she had intended.

'*Herein,*' Andreas's voice came low.

The room was spacious and uncluttered, bathed in half-light from blinds drawn at the windows. A vague hint of disinfectant clung in the air. But the surroundings were of no importance; all that Juli really saw was the man resting on the bed, propped up by pillows, wearing a navy blue robe over white silk pyjamas. His left leg was encased to the knee in plaster, and on his right temple a dressing showed pale against the darkness of tousled hair.

She closed the door softly and remained there, almost afraid to go near him. Now that she was here she felt horribly unsure of herself. 'Hello,' she managed. 'It's me. How are you?'

He didn't move, except to stiffen and tilt his head as if he doubted the evidence of his ears. 'Julienne?'

'Who else?'

'I thought you had gone,' Andreas said huskily. 'I thought you had left last night, with Marston.'

'How could I go without seeing you?' she asked through strangling distress, but controlled herself with an effort. 'How are you feeling? Are you in pain? The concussion—'

'It's nothing serious. A little headache. I was

154

lucky.'

Caught unawares by tears, she moved forward, blurting, 'I was so afraid! I couldn't have borne it if . . .' She stopped herself, hovering a few feet from the bed. 'Did they tell you Sara and Karl are safely back at Falkenruhe?'

'Yes, they told me.'

'And . . . you don't really think that I was a party to it, do you? I'm sorry for Sara, but I would never have agreed to help her in such a crazy scheme. I honestly didn't realise what she was doing.'

'I know,' he assured her gravely. 'I know. And how is Sara?'

Juli let out a sigh. 'She's all right. A bit subdued, maybe. I wouldn't say she's happy, but she seems ready to accept things as they are. I think she frightened herself yesterday. She . . . she appreciates what you've done for her. She asked me to say that she's sorry—and that she hopes you'll soon be well. It's a beginning.'

'Yes,' he said. 'Yes, it's good.'

'So what happens now?' she asked.

'We shall give her every opportunity to fulfil herself.'

'I meant . . .' She paused, biting her lip. 'I meant what happens about us?'

Again the silence lengthened. Then he said, 'Nothing has changed, Julienne.'

'*Everything* has changed!' she replied

155

passionately. 'I won't leave. I love you, Andreas, and you love me. I know you do.'

'Of course I love you! That's why . . .' His mouth closed like a trap on the words, but after a moment he added savagely, 'That's why I refuse to ask you to tie yourself to a blind man!'

Understanding—and utter disbelief—hit her like a drenching with icy water. 'You can't mean that!' she gasped. 'Is that what's been holding you back? That's insane! To waste your life, and mine . . . I thought you had more courage than that.'

The sally made him frown. 'Courage?'

'Only people who are afraid to face life run away from it! You're afraid of being hurt again—afraid to trust. I can understand that. I've felt the same myself. But you're so wrong, Andreas! Oh . . .' Unable to help herself, she sank down on the edge of the bed, curling her fingers round his, pleading with him. 'The other night you said you weren't a fairy-tale prince. Well, I'm not Cinderella, either. I'm an adult, independent, intelligent woman and I want a man I can love, and respect, and share with—a man who's not too proud to admit when he needs me. Anything else is of secondary importance. If we're together we'll have problems, I know that. But if we're apart I'll only be half alive. Is that what you want for me?'

The speech left her breathless and surprised at herself. She had never known she was capable of such vehemence.

In the silence, his fingers gripped hers painfully tight; then he said gruffly, 'No, it's not what I want, for you or for me. But . . . there is something else: I may not have the right to allow you to stay with me.'

'What does that mean?'

'It means . . . that I made a promise to someone.'

Oh, God! Juli felt as though her blood had turned suddenly to ice. Was there another woman in his life? 'To whom?' she managed.

'To Sir Charles Blake,' Andreas said.

The answer was so unexpected that it took a second to register in Juli's stunned mind. Then she breathed, 'Charles? My godfather? What does he have to do with this?'

'Everything,' Andreas said simply. 'The truth is . . . I promised him I would not interfere in your life.'

She stared at him, astounded. 'You did what? When?'

'Almost three years ago, soon after we met at Sharborough House.'

It was too much to take in. She shook her head, blinked hard. 'What?'

Letting out a long slow breath like a sigh, he lay back against his pillows, his hair dishevelled. His face was drawn in lines of weariness, but he held on to her hand as if the contact comforted him and through her concern for him Juli was aware of a warm current flowing between them.

'That night at Sharborough House,' he said, 'what happened between us was something rare, something special. I could not forget you. The memory stayed with me, sharp and clear, haunting me, until I knew I must do something about it.'

'It was the same for me,' Juli admitted huskily.

'Was it?' His fingers tightened in silent communion. 'I turned for help to Lady Sharborough, who told me your name and suggested that Sir Charles Blake might know where to find you. So I telephoned him. I told him I was trying to contact a photographer named Juli Blake and . . .' A wry smile curved his lips. 'Sir Charles became very angry. He refused to tell me anything. He knew of me— we had encountered one another in matters of business—and he knew that I was married. He evidently considered me a playboy. He appealed to my sense of honour. You were very young, he said. Very trusting and vulnerable. It was his duty to protect you from men like me, and if I had any decency . . .'

'I can imagine,' Juli sighed. 'Charles is a bit archaic at times. But . . . He told me he didn't know who you were! He pretended not even to know your name!'

'He was right to protect you,' Andreas said sadly. 'I was not free. I could offer you nothing but unhappiness. I knew that. So I decided to

158

put you out of my mind. I tried to make my marriage work. But, as you know, it was hopeless. The accident, the divorce ... I found myself with nothing left but the satisfaction of knowing that at least where you were concerned I had done the right thing. I did not forget, but I learned to make do with sweet memories of one enchanted evening. Nothing could spoil that.'

Juli reached her free hand to touch his face and let her fingers trace the strong line of his jaw, down his throat until her palm rested on the warm skin of his chest. 'So you would send me away, because of a promise you made three years ago when the circumstances were totally different.'

'No, *Liebling*.' His hand came to cover hers as he released another sigh. 'I renewed that promise to Sir Charles only a few weeks ago.'

'What? But why?'

'Because he asked it of me.' He grimaced, pulling his mouth awry. 'It began again when your friend Marston had his idea of using Falkenruhe as a background. I was not happy about it, I confess. I did not wish my privacy to be disturbed. However, I agreed. And then, with only a few hours' notice, we were told of a change of plan—a lady named Juli Blake was on her way. There was no time for me to avoid the meeting. I decided to pretend that I did not remember you. I hoped you might have forgotten me. But it soon became clear that you had not forgotten, any more than I had forgotten. It was still the same for us, still as strong, and growing stronger. Fate . . . Fate was determined to bring us together somehow.'

'Yes,' Juli agreed with a smile. 'You always said it was fate.'

He drew her hand to his lips, kissing her fingers. 'How hard I tried to resist it. I wanted you so badly, and yet without my sight I felt I had no right to ask anything of you. I had planned never to reveal that I remembered our first meeting. But the temptation was too great. There was a fight inside me—my love, and my need of you, at war with my sense of right and wrong. When you left, I thought it was a chance for us both to calm down and think. And then . . . that was when I heard again from Sir Charles. He was disturbed to know we had met again. He reminded me of my promise. He said that involvement with me could only hurt you, that I must see the only decent thing to do was to leave you alone.'

'Well, he had no right to interfere!' Juli said hotly. 'Especially without saying a word to me. Anyone would think I was a child.'

'To him, you are—a very dear child he would protect from the wicked world. Don't be angry with him, Julienne. He did it because he loves you. He wants only the best for you. Your happiness.'

'My happiness lies with you!'

Smiling, he reached with gentle fingers to

touch her face. 'How fierce you are. But you see now why I went away to America. You see why I sent the necklace—I wanted you to have something from me. I was being so noble staying away for your sake. Or so I thought. But in New York I could not concentrate. All I could think was that you were at Falkenruhe and I was not there with you. And then . . .'

The flow of his words stopped abruptly, as if he were reluctant to tell her what had happened next. Juli caught the hand that was caressing her face, drew it to her lips and kissed it, prompting, 'Tell me it all, Andreas. Please.'

A long sigh breathed out of him and he seemed to relax as he confessed, 'I met a doctor—an eye surgeon. When I told him my story he invited me to attend his clinic for an examination. I went the next day. Julienne . . . there is a new surgical technique, though it is still very experimental. There are no guarantees. Only a possibility of restoring some sight.'

'But that's wonderful!' Juli breathed. 'Why didn't you tell me?'

His grip on her hand had tightened painfully as he went on, 'I wanted to. I felt that if you were beside me I might find the courage to take this one last chance. That's why I came home. But when I heard Marston speaking of his love for you I knew I was being unfair. He is strong, and whole. All I had to offer was uncertainty, and perhaps disappointment in

161

the end. I had no right to ask you to share my troubles. So I said nothing. How changeable you must have thought me. Like a stupid schoolboy. Blowing hot, blowing cold. Knowing I should let you go, but unable to do so. Julienne . . . perhaps your godfather is right. Perhaps I am no good for you.'

'*I'll* decide what's good for me!' Juli said. 'Charles is . . .' She paused, sighing as she thought of her kindly godfather. 'Charles is afraid of losing me, that's what it is. He's afraid if I marry you he might never see me again. We'll just have to convince him he's wrong.'

'Indeed. We shall.'

The dryness of his tone made her realise what she had said and she flushed hotly. 'I sound as though I'm taking things for granted. I don't mean to. But you surely know that, if you're going to try for this new operation, I want to be there—I want to share it with you, however it turns out. Andreas, you're the one who believes in fate. If fate has decided we belong together . . .'

'Then why should we fight it?' he completed the thought, his thumb rubbing her knuckles as his voice went rusty with emotion. Julienne . . . when I woke up last night and thought that you were gone back to England . . . I wanted to die.'

'Ssh!' She laid her fingers across his lips, stopping the words, whispering, 'I haven't gone anywhere. I'm here. For as long as you need me.'

In a voice gone deep and gruff, he said slowly, 'I shall need you for always, my beautiful Julienne. *So wunderschön, mein Liebling.*' His fingers slid into her hair, his hands cupping her head, drawing her closer. She felt his breath warm on her skin as he murmured, '*Ich liebe dich,*' and then his mouth found hers and her being seemed to explode and melt in a great outpouring of love and longing and sheer dizzying joy.

All at once he twisted his head away and held her face pressed to his chest, where at the base of his throat her lips found a throbbing pulse under warm, smooth flesh. She could hear his heart pounding, feel him drawing deep breaths as he fought for control.

'I'll never leave you!' she muttered against his skin. 'Never!'

The only answer was a tightening of the arms that held her, so strong that she feared her bones might break. 'I am not strong enough to send you away,' he muttered. 'Not now. Not ever again. Julienne, I love you so much and I need you so much and I feel so . . .'

'Hush!' She laid her fingers across his lips, her eyes stinging in response to the sheen of tears in his. Tenderly she leaned to kiss his eyes, brushing his tears away with her lips, murmuring, 'It's all right, my darling. It's all right. I'm here.'

There would be problems ahead for them, she knew—the traumas of awaiting the operation and its results, the possibility of failure—Andreas would need her support whatever happened. But if they were together they could face what fate sent. If they had each other, nothing would seem so bad.

Also to be dealt with, Juli mused, were Sara's insecurity, Madame Ghislaine's pride and possessiveness, and Charles's fear of being left alone. As for young Karl . . . Perhaps, if he had a cousin, or two, or three, then Madame would relax her vigilance and Sara might feel less pressured . . .

It could help to ease several problems at one fell swoop.

'Why are you smiling?' Andreas asked, his tender, inquisitive fingers following the curve of her lips.

'I was just thinking. I know you decided you were never going to have children, but it does seem a shame. I mean, Karl could do with some playmates, and there's masses of room at the castle.'

'Masses,' Andreas agreed, smiling peacefully. 'And if that's a proposal, I accept. Though I wonder, can this really be the same Miss Prim—the lady who didn't allow her heart to have its way?'

'The very same,' Juli said, nestling against him. 'Except that this time, beautiful stranger, I don't intend ever to let you go.'